indie girl

Kavita Daswani

SIMON PULSE
New York · London · Toronto · Sydney

SIMON PULSE
An imprint of Simon & Schuster Children's Publishing Division
1230 Avenue of the Americas, New York, NY 10020
Copyright © 2007 by Kavita Daswani
All rights reserved, including the right of reproduction
in whole or in part in any form.
SIMON PULSE and colophon are registered trademarks of
Simon & Schuster, Inc.
Designed by Jessica Sonkin
The text of this book was set in Aldine721 BT.
Manufactured in the United States of America
First Simon Pulse edition October 2007
2 4 6 8 10 9 7 5 3 1
Library of Congress Control Number 2007927644
ISBN-13: 978-1-4169-4892-6
ISBN-10: 1-4169-4892-9

For my sweet boys, Jahan and Nirvan.
May you always know how loved you are.

ACKNOWLEDGMENTS

I would like to express my profound gratitude to my editor at Simon Pulse, Sangeeta Mehta, for seeing this book in her mind before the first word had even been written. Her smart, insightful, and enthusiastic input was as crucial as me sitting down every day to write. This book would not have happened without her.

My thanks to my agent, Jodie Rhodes, who remains as dedicated and loyal and tenacious as the day she signed me. A big thank-you to my sister, Mansha, who spent a chunk of her last vacation reading the manuscript and giving me the benefit of her keen eye.

And last, in acknowledgment of Shirdi Baba, who watches over my family.

one

Today, I would be meeting the woman whom I was convinced would change my life.

In approximately one hour and twenty-five minutes, Aaralyn Taylor would glide into our school's assembly hall.

There, poised against a lectern at the Meadow Lake High School in Agoura, in the suburbs of Los Angeles, she would address the crowd about her experiences as the editor of *Celebrity Style*, the hottest celebrity and fashion magazine around. Then, after enrapturing her audience, she would wait to take questions.

I, of course, would ask the most insightful and thought-provoking ones. She wouldn't be able to help noticing my profound intelligence. And then, as the crowd would start to disperse, she would signal to me to meet her in the foyer, and would proceed to tell me that I was the smartest fifteen-year-old she had ever met. I would reach into my Kate Spade striped canvas knockoff, from which hung a good-luck charm in the shape of the Hindu elephant god, Ganesha, and fish out a bright pink folder containing my pretend-reports from the catwalks, my perceptive analyses of recent runway events that I had seen on the Internet, if not in person. Aaralyn Taylor would then offer me the summer internship I had applied for at the magazine she had founded three years ago and that she had turned into a huge success.

Today, a beautiful March day when the chill of winter had passed and we were in the full bloom of spring, was going to be one I would never forget.

I turned once again to look at the clock.

"Indira! Are you paying attention?"

Mr. Fogerty, my chemistry instructor, was suddenly standing in front of me, his four-foot-five frame seeming even more stunted now that I was perched on a high, round stool.

"Mass and mole relationships," he said, his small red nose covered with tiny whiteheads. "It was your assigned reading last night. I take it you're familiar with the chapter?"

"Yes," I lied. It was uncharacteristic of me. I *always* did my homework, even if it was sometimes at the very last minute, as I was buttering my toast at breakfast. My parents would have been mortified to learn that instead of poring over chemistry books the night before I had been rereading the last four issues of *Celebrity Style*, prepping for my life-altering exchange with Aaralyn today. As far as I was concerned, mass and mole could have been the name of a Guatemalan appetizer.

"So let's start with you then," he said, a look of smug satisfaction on his face. "Perhaps, Indira, you can enlighten us as to the distinction between molecular mass and formula mass?"

There was a lot that I didn't like about Mr. Fogerty. But the fact that he insisted on calling me "Indira" was at the top of the list. Granted, it was the name I had been given at birth, the one that was inked on my birth certificate and on the crisp pages of my American passport. I might have been able to live with it if my last name was not Konkipuddi. It was such a mouthful that most people gave up midway. In elementary school, I had been teased mercilessly because of my odd-sounding last name, which was perfectly common in India. The other kids used to call me "Conk" and "Conkers" and "Pudding." So I started calling myself "Indie," as if in doing so I was helping them forget that I had such a cumbersome surname. Indie was short and sweet and memorable. It was what I called myself, who I felt I was.

When I had started complaining about how old-fashioned my first name was, my father told me that in deciding what to call his firstborn child, it had been his hope that I would embody all that he admired about his native land and the other Indira—Indira Gandhi—who once led it. He wanted me to be strong, virtuous, compassionate, intellectual.

And while he had originally wanted me to choose what he constantly would refer to as a "noble profession"—something in medicine or engineering or government—his views had started to change recently when his nephew Naresh had landed a six-figure job in New York in the digital media arena. Every time my father would speak to Naresh, my cousin would use terms like "interfacing" and "multimedia."

Although my father had yet to fully understand what my cousin did exactly, the fact that Naresh was able to send a substantial amount of money to his parents in India every month, and had paid in cash for a loft in Soho, had convinced my father that there lay an entire world beyond the borders of law and the sciences, the kind of vocations that he and other Indian parents had always held in the highest esteem.

"Indira!" Mr. Fogerty called out again. "Are you with us?"

I opened my mouth, prepared to make something up about molecular structures. But fortunately the bell rang, books were slammed shut, and bags swiped off tables.

Only two more periods to go.

There was a feature article I had once glanced at in a magazine, which was in the office of my father's neurological practice, about what children dreamed of becoming when they grew up. According to the report, boys who once longed to be soldiers or astronauts or pilots would instead end up becoming insurance executives or chefs or investment bankers. Similarly, girls who saw themselves as movie stars and nurses and missionaries would end up raising children full-time or becoming management consultants or trial lawyers. The point of the feature was to highlight that what most children say they will do professionally as adults is almost always vastly different to the reality. As the article concluded, the practicalities of life often got in the way.

But despite what I had read, I knew in my heart of hearts that the career I had seen for myself would definitely, no matter what, happen for me. When I had decided, at age eleven, that I would one day become a fashion reporter, there had been no doubt in my mind that I would somehow get there. Even if nobody in my family could understand my fascination with clothes and shoes and supermodels, my commitment to the cause never wavered.

I can remember exactly when it happened. It was a sweltering hot summer, the first week of school vacation, and I was beyond bored. Some of my friends were in summer camp, while others had rented vacation houses in Mexico or Costa Rica or Santa Barbara. My parents had opted not to go that route, choosing instead to spend time with my baby brother, Dinesh, and myself, doing fun, family things in the comfort and convenience of our own home, with the exception of some day trips on the side.

But my father was suddenly asked to speak at an important conference in the fall, and needed to spend endless days during *my* vacation preparing for it. As if that wasn't enough of a disappointment, my mother got immersed in some volunteer project that involved collecting clothes and toys to send to charities in India.

All of a sudden, those plans to visit Legoland, Disneyland, and the Monterey Bay Aquarium disappeared, leaving me with nothing but a basket of Barbie dolls and endless hours of Nickelodeon to keep me occupied.

After I had spent yet another afternoon complaining about having "nothing to do," my mother took me to the local crafts store and asked me to take my pick: I could choose from scrapbooking, candle making, or quilting. There were balsa wood airplanes to be put together, stained-glass kits to fiddle with, glistening multicolored beads to string into necklaces.

But nothing captivated me.

On the way home, we stopped at the library so my mother could pick up a copy of the latest John Grisham. While we were waiting in line, me clutching *Are You There God? It's Me, Margaret*, which I had really wanted to reread, something caught my eye on the top of a donated pile of books someone had left on the counter. I shoved the book I was holding under my arm, reached out for the one I had just seen, and held it firmly, transfixed by the image on the front. The black-and-white picture fascinated me; it was of a fashion model standing in a large plastic bubble that was floating down what looked like the Seine. She was gazing outward, looking prim and elegant in a checked suit. I turned the book around, and there she was again, in the same bubble, but this time on a dirt-strewn road. She was wearing gloves and a long dress, her dark hair swept off her face.

"I want this," I said to my mother, who plucked it out of my hands to look at it.

"*Melvin Sokolsky: Seeing Fashion*," she said, announcing the name of the book and its author. "I've never heard of him."

"Yes, but I want it," I said.

The book had yet to be cataloged and entered into the system, but the librarian told me that if I came back the next day, she would have it set aside for me.

That night, through dinner and even in my sleep, those pictures didn't leave my head.

First thing the next morning, after my brother and I accompanied my mother on her clothes-collecting mission, I dragged her back to the library to pick up the book. I had my eyes glued to it all the way home and for the rest of the day. As I discovered, Sokolsky was a fashion photographer from the 1960s who took pictures for magazines like *Vogue* and *Harper's Bazaar*. The photographs were a collection of his work over the years, each one more mesmerizing than the last; there were shots of girls in gowns dancing on giant chairs, and women in bright-colored suits suspended from strings, like marionettes. I studied all of them, memorizing not just the setting but the clothes, staring at the hair and makeup, taking note of the designers whose clothes the models were wearing. At dinner that night, I kept the book next to me, on the table.

"What *is* that you've been reading all day?" asked my father, who had been working on his speech in his office at home.

"A book on fashion," I said. "The first one I've ever seen. I love it."

"Well, at least it's something to keep you occupied," my mother announced wearily as she transported a tin of hot *chapatis* from the kitchen. "Finally, one whole day in which you've not told me that you are bored."

That's how it began. This was before I was really familiar with Google, so I had no choice but to actually leave my house to find out more. I went back to the library to see if there were any more fashion books, and checked out anything I could get my hands on. When I had exhausted all those possibilities, I asked my mother to take me to Borders and Barnes & Noble, where I sat in a chair leafing through encyclopedias on fashion and books on fashion history that I knew I could never afford to buy, my mother hovering nearby checking out the arrivals on the New Fiction table. I went all the way back to Egypt in 3000 BC, which, according to the weightier books on the subject said, was where fashion began. And I slowly charted its evolution through the ages, through ancient cultures, to arrive at where we were today.

All of a sudden, history was interesting to me; if I didn't know the difference between Mayans and Etruscans before, I knew it now. As I left Borders one humid afternoon, I stopped by the magazine section, where I picked up a copy of *InStyle*. I leafed through the pages, gazing at the silk bustiers and taffeta gowns, the hip-hugging denim capris and leather halterneck dresses worn by rich, famous, and beautiful people. I loved staring at the clothes in the pictures, wanting to soak in the details of each and every one.

It was that summer that I decided that fashion was going to be my life.

Now, at fifteen, my ambitions were utterly serious. Girls my age loved to troll through the mall, checking out the cool clothes in store windows. That was all fine and fun. But as far as I saw it, the study of fashion was a serious academic exercise. While the other girls in my class looked at "The Red Carpet" section of *Us Magazine*, I perused the contents of *The St. James Fashion Encyclopedia: A Survey of*

Style from 1945 to the Present. When they were off listening to the new Gwen Stefani album, I would be examining every item of clothing she was wearing in her videos, guessing which designer she had chosen and why, writing lengthy dissertations for myself about how her fashion choices reflected her mind and music.

I put as much thought into fashion as my friends did when they were cramming for geometry or biology or English. That's why I loved *Celebrity Style* so much. It took fashion as seriously as I did. It didn't do what other magazines did—stalking famous people, writing about their drug addictions and alcoholic binges. It didn't talk down to young readers, like so many of those teen magazines did. It was about fashion, yes. But as I told my mother countless times, it was frivolous in a *good* way. Few magazines could claim such a virtue. Yes, there were beautiful pictures and glamorous clothes, but I loved how it was put together. It was really about *style.* And because I was so in love with the subject, I could talk for an hour about Donna Karan's signature look or the resurgence of Pucci or what defined London street style. I *cared* about it.

Fashion was my life. And today, after staving off sleep during algebra and being breathed on in class by Mrs. Mok, who had the worst case of halitosis ever, I was finally going to start living it.

two

I skipped the last five minutes of phys ed so I could hit the showers early, beating out the lines that would invariably start forming outside the curtained-off cubicles. It was my least favorite subject anyway: The problem with exercise, I had decided, was that it involved movement. Whenever my mother was in an especially generous mood, I would take advantage of it by asking her to write a note for Mrs. Mok, specifying that my allergies were acting up, that I was wheezing and puffing and couldn't *possibly* jog around the campus again. My mother might have known that this wasn't true, and that perhaps it didn't reflect well on my doctor father, to have a daughter who always claimed some ailment or another. But my mother was a very practical sort: As long as I didn't miss "real classes" as she called them, skipping phys ed on occasion was fine. After all, being able to sprint a couple of miles or score goals wasn't going to help me get into an Ivy League college, was it? But today, I had decided to go for it, figuring that maybe a bout of exercise would lend a nice blush to my cheeks and a shine to my eyes before my life-changing moment with Aaralyn Taylor.

Still, my lack of interest in the exercise discipline, combined with the love of my mother's homemade *idli sambar*, accounted for the roll of flab I had around my waist and that hovered on my upper thighs, parts of me that my irritating younger brother would describe as "jiggly bits."

And I had to confess that there were moments when I would almost succumb to the desperation to be thin that lived in the air around me and that was everywhere I looked. There were at least three other girls I knew of in my school who chewed gum all day because it was the only thing that made them feel less hungry. I couldn't imagine forgoing my mother's *dosa* for a packet of Dentyne. There were rumors that Ashli, a brunette who was a math whiz although she looked like she could be a model, would routinely throw up after lunch, just so she would never have to worry about zipping up her True Religion jeans. Anybody considered even remotely fat or pudgy was immediately discounted as a "loser," even if they were sweet and smart. I had tried, ever since I started high school, not to buy into it, to try and be comfortable with who I was. But I would be the first to admit that it was not always easy, that I had pushed away my mac-and-cheese in the cafeteria more than once, that I had vowed to start that watermelon diet on Monday, but had given up as soon as I smelled my mother's spices.

So thank heaven I knew how to dress. With the right cut of top and jeans, I had grown pretty good at camouflaging the parts of myself I most disliked.

Today, the day my life was going to change, I had carefully picked out a pair of cords, my favorite cap-sleeved cotton tee, and a nifty blazer with burnished chrome buttons. Gazing into the steamed-up mirror, I slicked back the golden highlights in my short hair, the color of which had made my parents cringe when I first came home with them a few weeks ago. It had been inconceivable that a black-haired Indian girl could carry off such pale streaks, but I somehow had managed to accomplish it, and even my parents eventually had to agree that I "looked nice." The tiny diamond I wore in my right nostril sparkled beneath a spotlight overhead. When I had first started high school, all the girls had *oohed* and *ahhed* about my innate fashion sense. I decided not to tell them that every woman in my family had had a nose piercing as soon as she "approached womanhood" as my mother had nauseatingly called it, and that fashion had nothing to do with it. On my lips I rubbed some bronze-colored gloss, and feathered some mascara onto my lashes. I spritzed on the Shalimar perfume I had taken from my mother's dressing table, wanting desperately to smell like a grown-up. Then I took a slim chartreuse-colored *dupatta* and wove it through my belt loops, adding just a touch of ethnicity without looking like I was going to a Bengali religious festival. On my left wrist, surrounding the Timex I had found on eBay, were four mirrored bangles, their slim wooden bases knocking against each other. My mother had bought them for me during a recent grocery-shopping visit to "Little India" in Artesia, more than an hour's drive from our house, but as close to going back to Calcutta as possible without actually having to get on a plane. When my mother had first brought them home, I had grimaced at their ultra-Indianness. But now, combined with bootleg corduroys, Nepalese beads around my neck, and pointy-toed Payless shoes on my feet, they looked perfect.

I stepped back, wishing that the school would at least invest in a full-length mirror in the girls' changing room. I looked at myself up and down, reminding myself again why I coveted clothes so much. In the right things, like I was wearing today, I could shine. I could stand out and be distinctive. Fashion, in that sense, was really the only thing that helped me make any kind of a mark.

Now, I just had to hope that Aaralyn Taylor, discriminating fashionista that she was, would agree.

The auditorium was still being set up when I arrived. Brown plastic chairs were being wheeled out and stacked in rows, about twenty in a line, stretching all the way back in the hall. Aaralyn Taylor wasn't due to arrive for another fifteen minutes. The idea was for the assembly hall to be packed with eager listeners before she got there. Given her celebrity status and the fact that today's visit was the highlight of Career Week, there was no reason it wouldn't be. Guests from the previous day had included someone from NASA and a transport official from Los Angeles County, neither of whom had interested me very much. The following day, there would be talks given by a Silicon Valley executive and a political blogger, both of which had potential. But this encounter with someone who sat front row at all the biggest fashion shows, who regularly chatted on the phone with Nicole Kidman's stylist or had personal shopping expeditions at Barneys: Well, how could anyone *not* want to come hear her? Aaralyn had become almost as famous as the stars who appeared in the pages of her magazine. I had seen her on TV, on the red carpet at all the award shows, being interviewed about her dress and jewels as if she were a nominee herself. She was the Anna Wintour of the West Coast, someone whose glamorous looks and coveted closet and access to huge movie stars put her in the same league as them.

But there was another far more compelling reason for me to be here.

The other week, tacked onto the bulletin board in the

College Counseling Center, was a flyer that made my head spin.

There, a few months before the end of semester and the start of summer break, counselors would post potential internships at local businesses that students might be interested in taking on over the summer. There were also babysitting jobs and lots of assistant positions to entertainment-industry types who lived out here in suburbia. But there were often a number of service jobs as well—sales positions in neighborhood boutiques or cashier postings in restaurants and cafés. I had gone along in the hopes of checking out potential listings for anything to do with fashion: Maybe the Gap or Victoria's Secret in the mall closest to my home needed some help over the summer. Maybe I could spray perfume on people who walked through the beauty floor at Nordstrom; it was beauty and not fashion, but at least I'd be close to gorgeous clothes. There would have to be *something* for me.

And that's when I saw it.

A pale green sheet of paper and, on it, in medium-size gray font some words that had made me almost faint with excitement.

Summer Internship Available at Celebrity Style. Top US national celebrity and fashion magazine needs a bright, talented, personable intern for the teen fashion department. The position entails receiving and returning samples, helping to manage the fashion closet, answering phones, and general admin duties. For the right person, there may be opportunities to attend product launches and accompany senior fashion staff to interviews and photo shoots. Familiarity with Mac OS X is crucial. Minimal pay, but a great opportunity for someone who is interested in fashion and journalism. To apply, please write no more than 200 words explaining why you are the right person for the job. Please submit all applications by March 15. Our Human Resources Department will inform the successful applicant by June 15. The internship will begin on July 1 and run for six weeks. Must be 16 years of age by July 1 to be eligible. No phone calls, please.

This was it. This was everything I had ever wanted. I couldn't tear myself away from the flyer. I would qualify well before July 1. *Celebrity Style* wanted me!

When I had gone home that afternoon, I barely spoke to my mother before racing upstairs to my computer. All I had been able to think about all day was how I would wow the people at the magazine, Aaralyn Taylor especially, not just with my enormous knowledge of and passion for the subject of fashion, but also for my reliability, efficiency, and punctuality. There was no way

I couldn't get this job. I would know each and every item of clothing on sight. And as for accompanying a senior fashion editor on an interview or photo shoot—I would be knowledgeable and smart and would do the magazine proud. I was *perfect* for it. I just knew in my heart that nobody would be able to do this better than me. I didn't care that it was in West Los Angeles, and that I would have to take three buses and spend two hours getting there. It was a matter of fate that I had come into the College Counseling Center that day and seen the flyer. My parents had always taught me to believe in destiny, and here it was, staring me in the face.

I peered intently at the screen. There was an application that had to be downloaded, printed out, filled in, and mailed back to a street address in Beverly Hills.

There wasn't anyone who would read this and who would doubt my sincerity. Aaralyn Taylor, I had decided, must have been like me once. My words would resonate with her. She would see a kindred soul in me.

I thought of all that now, as I hung around the assembly hall waiting for the talk to begin. I had already sent in my application, *before* the deadline. I guess they had to give everyone a fair shot, but I was sure that my bid for the job was on the top of a big pile of them on Aaralyn Taylor's desk, and that she had drawn a gold star on it and stuck on a Post-it note to call me.

I looked around for my best friend, Kim, whose

parents were Korean and, like my own, traditional but trying to keep up with the times. I finally caught sight of her down the long corridor, her blunt hair swinging from side to side as she waved and made her way toward me. She was the spitting image of her mother. Mrs. Cho was small and slender, her cheekbones high, her skin porcelain. She had always reminded me of a little doll. Kim had inherited her mother's pretty if rather bland looks, but had elected to give herself a bit of an edge with some rather unusual fashion choices. One weekend she had dyed her bangs pink. Another, she had paid for an airbrush tattoo across her upper arm. Last week, she came to school wearing a vintage Hermès tie and baggy gray pants, looking for all the world like an Asian Annie Hall.

"Wow, you look fab," she said. "I skipped phys ed. Cramps. How was it?"

"Look, we need to sit up front, okay?" I said, ignoring her question. "I want Aaralyn Taylor to be looking right at me."

"Shouldn't be a problem," she answered. "Nobody's here yet. As soon as these guys finish setting up the room, we can go in and sit down. Nervous?"

"Kind of," I replied. "I know you think I'm crazy, but this is the moment I've been waiting for. "

"Indie, you think I don't know that you've saved every issue of that magazine? That you keep folders crammed with pictures of each season's must-haves? I love pretty clothes as much as the next girl. But you're insane."

"Yeah, but you love me anyway," I said, grabbing her by the hand and dragging her into the auditorium.

I had told my mother to pick me up a little later than usual today. I had warned her that I would probably be deep in conversation with Aaralyn Taylor when she got there, and that I might need a few extra minutes to wrap things up. My mother, as she always did, rolled her eyes and proceeded to ladle out the homemade yogurt sweetened with wildflower honey she was serving for breakfast.

She had asked me why I had skipped the NASA speaker the day before, and why I wasn't scheduled to be in on the Silicon Valley insider the following afternoon. I wasn't sure how to explain it to her. Somehow, between the heaping spoonfuls of cut papayas drizzled with lime juice and the jam-smeared croissants that followed, I didn't find the opportunity to inform my mother that the main reason I wanted to attend Aaralyn Taylor's talk was so I could meet her in person before I went to work for her. Summer break wasn't too far off, and I wanted to have something lined up—something more enjoyable than taking appointments at the dentist's office, like Kim was planning. I wanted to spend those glorious summer days going to interviews and fashion shoots and product launches all around town. It was going to be fabulous, and I was going to be part of it.

"It's nothing, Mom," I said, responding to my mother's concerns. "I just think she'll be interesting, that's all. And you know how I much I like fashion."

three

I could barely contain my excitement.

Yet, at the moment that the talk should have been starting, there was still no sign of Aaralyn Taylor.

In the corner of the podium, I spotted the school's career counselor, Ms. Jennings, in deep discussion with Mr. Baker, the vice principal. They looked flushed and anxious. I glanced around the hall, and noticed that only about a quarter of the seats were filled. A sense of alarm started to rise in my belly. Maybe Aaralyn Taylor wasn't coming. Maybe she was called away on some exotic photo shoot in Tahiti or had a last-minute interview with Chloë Sevigny or broke a heel on one of her Blahniks. Whatever the reason, I would be devastated if she didn't show up.

"Let me go find out what's going on," said Kim, rising from her seat, obviously in her element as a seeker of truth of all things high school–related. She returned a few minutes later, a look of mild amusement on her face.

"Drama," she said with a flourish of the hand. "Seems

that a hoax e-mail went out canceling today's event. I didn't get it. Did you? How bizarre! So that's why there are so many no-shows, and now the diva won't get out of her car because she was told that it wasn't a full house. She's furious!"

"So now what?" I asked, getting sucked into the saga of it all.

"Mr. Baker is going out there again to try and talk her into coming in anyway. She wanted to reschedule, but he's telling her that there are enough people who made it. So it's up in the air for now."

Fifteen anxious minutes later, Ms. Jennings strolled onto the podium, her face more relaxed, and stood in front of a tall microphone.

"Hello everyone, and thank you for coming," she said. "There's been a little mix-up this afternoon, so we appreciate your patience as we tried to smooth things out. Anyway, we are delighted that Ms. Aaralyn Taylor, the founder, publisher, and editor of *Celebrity Style*, the most successful fashion and celebrity magazine of the last few years, has agreed to come and talk to us about the business of fashion reporting."

I turned to Kim, and gleefully punched my fist in the air.

"Please give a welcoming round of applause to Ms. Aaralyn Taylor," Ms. Jennings beseeched.

I clapped wildly, the sound of my palms slapping

together louder than everyone around me. I straightened my back, not wanting to miss a second of Aaralyn's entrance, needing to catch every movement she made.

She strode in through the right-hand door to the auditorium, the one that led straight to the podium. She was even more striking in person than in the picture on her magazine's masthead. Her long reddish-blond hair was pulled back into a high ponytail. She was dressed in a cropped tweed lavender jacket, which I could immediately identify as from Chanel's new spring collection, and wide-cut white linen pants. On her feet were high-heeled mules in the same color as the jacket. A thick silver charm bracelet hung off one tiny wrist, large silver hoops gleamed in her ears. She was pristine.

"She looks pissed," Kim whispered as I nudged her to be quiet. "She probably gets packed houses wherever she goes and now she's here at this pathetic showing."

"Hush!" I hissed. "It's about to start."

Aaralyn positioned herself in front of the microphone, took a sip of water from a glass set on the lectern in front of her, and started to speak.

"First, I'd like to thank Doris Jennings and Matthew Baker for inviting me today. And of course, I wouldn't be here at all if it weren't for the fact that I have a personal connection with someone at this school."

My heart stopped. Someone here at school knew Aaralyn Taylor *personally*? I turned around to face the aisle adjacent to mine, following Aaralyn's gaze in that general direction. There, I saw a shiny blonde head nod, the pretty face underneath it beaming proudly, a casual wave of a slender wrist. I knew that girl.

"Yes," Aaralyn continued, now finally smiling. "Brooke Carlyle—who I'm sure is well-known here for her impeccable wardrobe and overall genius, is my niece. I guess a passion for fashion runs in the genes!"

I had never spoken to Brooke Carlyle—or rather, she had never spoken to me. She was the leader of a pack that Kim called "the blonde bubbleheads," even if they weren't really bubbleheads. They were girls with such hefty allowances that they only wore Marc Jacobs and Zac Posen, came to school in their father's Hummer and mother's Jaguar, and were all named Britney or Skylar or Tiffany. Or Brooke.

But everything made sense now. Why, indeed, would Aaralyn Taylor pick this particular school to deliver a career address? And now that I thought about it: Why was she advertising for a summer intern here, of all places? Because of Brooke as well? I suppose, in an odd way, I had much to thank Brooke Carlyle for. I should have been grateful, but I suddenly started to feel uncomfortable; all this time I thought I was the only person here who had such a strong affinity with *Celebrity Style*. But now, just a few seats away from me, someone else had one that was far more concrete than mine.

"Anyway, on to the matter at hand," said Aaralyn.

In a crisp, no-nonsense tone, she reminisced briefly about being fifteen, when she decided that she would one day leave her hometown of Bakersfield and live in a big, bright city: New York, San Francisco, or Los Angeles.

"And so I came to LA when I was fresh out of college, worked as an assistant at one of the big talent agencies, got some real hands-on experience at two other entertainment and fashion magazines, and then finally started *Celebrity Style*. I'd say going to college really helped me because I got a management degree, and that's what I needed most when it came time to set up my own magazine. But I also really took the time to learn about fashion—the business of it, as well as what great design really is. It's not just a superficial thing for me. I take it very seriously. Now, I've been told that we're giving magazines like *Vogue* a run for their money!"

I was entranced. She talked about how she struggled in the beginning, setting up the magazine using a loan from a wealthy uncle. It took her five years to pay him back. She talked about how hard it was to get advertisers to come on board, how she had to personally convince them that she knew what she was doing.

"There were so many magazines," she said, looking suddenly wistful. "There were tabloids and there were the gorgeous fashion and celebrity glossies. The newsstands were packed. Everyone told me that the last thing the world needed was another fashion magazine. But the more they said that, the more I wanted to prove them wrong."

The turning point had been about two years ago, when she landed an exclusive about one of New York's most important designers doing an inexpensive collection for a discount chain, and enlisting an A-list actress to be his model. She had heard about it from an old college friend who worked for the store, and so got her hands on the story well before her competitors.

"I scooped them," she said, a smile reappearing on her face. "And it felt good. Suddenly, everyone was talking about us. That's all it took—publishing a great story in advance of anyone else. We haven't looked back."

She paused for a moment, said "thank you" and looked around the room. Mr. Baker approached the microphone, which was Aaralyn's cue to step back.

"That was a very illuminating and interesting talk," Mr. Baker said, his Adam's apple bobbing up and down his thick neck. "Now, I'm certain some of our students are eager to ask questions. I'm happy to open the floor."

I turned to look around and saw just two hands up, way at the back. Brooke hadn't raised her hand either. Some show of family loyalty that was, I thought. Kim pushed my elbow upward, hoisting my arm into the air. I had come in with a list of questions engraved onto my brain, but now that I was here, I couldn't think of any of them. But it was too late; thanks to Kim, my hand now hovered in the space above my head.

"Yes, in the front," said Mr. Baker. "Maybe you'd like to stand up so we can all hear you?"

I trembled as I rose to my feet. Aaralyn was looking straight at me, her face stony, her eyes a cold blue.

"Yes?" she said, forcing a smile.

"Um, er, what would you say it took to really make it in the world of fashion journalism?" I asked, now remembering one of the questions I had practiced for days. "Would you say there is one quality that a person should have to get ahead in the field? Talent? A good eye? The ability to write concisely?"

Aaralyn briefly closed her eyes, before pressing her mouth closer to the microphone.

"It's very competitive," she said. "There are thousands of young girls who dream of covering the shows and meeting movie stars. And, truthfully, it takes more than talent and writing skills. It's a bit like Hollywood," she said, smiling faintly. "Most of the time, it's all about who you know. In fact, sometimes it seems that who you know trumps any actual ability. It's a sad fact of the entertainment and media business." She looked out at the audience. "Next question?"

I suddenly got a funny feeling in the pit of my stomach. Was Aaralyn telling me not to bother, that unless I had the right connections, I didn't have a shot of making it? As I thought about it some more, I realized that that didn't even make sense. If that's how she really felt, then why bother to advertise for an intern? If only people who knew the right people ever got those jobs, then why seek outside that circle? Her words left me cold. It wasn't what I expected to hear. I stood, immobile, rooted to the spot.

"But . . . but," I started to stammer. I wanted to correct Aaralyn Taylor. I wanted to tell her what my father had always told me: that hard work and being conscientious and loving what you did were the keys to success. He had never said anything about having connections.

Mr. Baker interjected before I had a chance to say anything else, and moved on to the next question. I nodded and sat down. Between Aaralyn's depressing answer and the fact that there was one girl at this school who would always know her better than me, no matter what happened here today, the enthusiasm I had harbored for weeks had suddenly fizzled.

I had come here hoping that Aaralyn would tell me that intelligence and determination—both of which I knew I had plenty of—would take me to where I wanted to go, would guarantee me an opportunity to work in this field. I had wanted her to reassure me that I wasn't wasting my time and dreaming of impossible goals, that it didn't matter if my father was a neurosurgeon and my mother a homemaker and that their combined fashion knowledge amounted to which fabrics would shrink in the clothes dryer. I wanted to hear that it was irrelevant that we lived in the middle of suburbia, on the pretty paved streets of Agoura, forty miles away from Beverly Hills and Robertson Boulevard and Melrose, and thousands of miles from New York City—all the places where fashion really happened.

And I realized then, with a sobering certainty, that being on a first-name basis with one of the salesgirls at my local Old Navy wouldn't qualify as an "inside track." For all the lack of any contacts and connections to the fashion world, I might as well have proclaimed my desire to be the first teenager on the moon.

"That was fun," Kim said, gathering her things from under her seat, at the end of the talk. I was still staring at the podium, where Aaralyn was talking quietly with Ms. Jennings and Mr. Baker, their heads bowed together as if in a football huddle, shielding their conversation from the students slowly filing out. Brooke was standing nearby, clinging to her aunt, both of them pretty and shiny, not a crease to be found between them.

I stood up to leave, looking at the clock and realizing that I still had ten minutes before my mother would be waiting for me outside, her nose in the book she always carried around for times when the lines at the bank and post office and supermarket checkout were longer than expected. She only managed to read a few pages a day, but using just those tiny slivers of time, when most people would be daydreaming or checking their voice mail or deleting junk messages on their BlackBerry, my mother was able to make her way through just about every novel on the Man Booker Prize short list. I had always admired that about her—her thoughtful use of time, the way she embraced the wider world without necessarily having to feel like she had to be loud and bold about it.

"You know, I think I'm going to go up and talk to her," I said. My determination had suddenly returned.

"What?" Kim asked.

"I'm never going to have this opportunity again," I said. "It's now or never. She said you needed to have the right contacts to work in this business. I don't have those and never will. I'm never going to be Brooke Carlyle. All I want to do is work at her magazine over the summer. So given the fact that I have nothing to lose, I'm going to go up to Aaralyn Taylor and ask her for that job."

four

When I approached her, I couldn't summon up the courage to actually talk to her. For all my resolute determination, when push came to shove, I just wanted to run in the opposite direction. It was like there was a glass wall around Aaralyn Taylor that could only be shattered by people smarter, savvier, prettier than me.

I watched as she picked up the metallic leather Fendi clutch that lay on a chair at the back of the podium, and kissed her niece good-bye. Then, accompanied by Ms. Jennings and Mr. Baker, she made her way right past me, down the corridor and toward a long, shiny, black car that was waiting outside for her. I followed them out, feeling a bit like a stalker, but relieved that so far, none of them had noticed me. At the limo, my teachers said good-bye to our visitor, and she turned toward her car, a door held open by a driver in a smart blue suit.

She slid into the car and slammed the door shut. The engine started, and the driver began pulling out, getting ready to turn around and head out the large gate that served as the main entrance to our school. For a second, I didn't know what to do. I couldn't let her get away. I let my bag fall to the ground and, spurred on by some senseless desperation, began running after the car, waving madly as it slowly moved away.

"Miss Taylor, hello, Miss Taylor!" I yelled. "Please come back! I need to ask you something! Please!"

The car suddenly stopped. I swore under my breath. I walked closer and waited as the tinted rear window slowly slid down. Aaralyn's perfect face appeared through it.

"Yes? What's wrong? What do you want?" she asked.

"Miss Taylor, it's *me. Indie.*" I waited for a look of recognition to appear on her face. My application for the internship must have been on the top of that pile! She MUST know my name by now! I just had to jog her memory!

"*Who?*" she said, looking irritated. "Look, I have no idea who you are or what you want, but I really must go."

"I applied for the internship," I said, my voice trembling. "I sent in my application two weeks ago. Maybe you didn't receive it?"

"Oh, *that,*" she said. "Look, I'm not really sure." she said. "It's really in the hands of our Human Resources Department. I'm too busy to be involved in that process. Sorry." She was about to roll up the window again.

My heart felt like it was about to plunge into the soles

of my shoes. I had met the deadline! There wasn't anybody anywhere more suited for the job—internally or externally! Surely someone would have brought my application to her attention?

"You have no idea what a fan I am, Miss Taylor," I said, taking another tack. "I *study* your magazines. You are such an inspiration to me." I was aware that I sounded like a lovesick groupie, but the words just tumbled out of my mouth.

"Thank you," she said politely. "But if you don't mind, I have another meeting to get to."

The driver turned around to look at me, rolled his eyes in my general direction, and then went back to his steering wheel.

"Is there *any* chance I can intern with you over the summer? Please? I know a lot about fashion, ask me anything, go on, you'll see." I knew I sounded unattractively desperate, but couldn't stop talking.

Aaralyn sighed and looked away, pausing for a minute.

"Do you have any idea how many letters I get every week from girls like you who want to come and work for me?" she asked. "Hundreds. I don't even open them. There's no point. They're mostly from kids who think that just because they are wearing the latest little trend they have what it takes to be a fashion writer. They don't."

That's when I started crying. The stress of the past few days had finally gotten to me. But it was also the realization that, in Aaralyn Taylor's eyes, I was nobody special, nobody unique. Indeed, I was nobody at all.

"I'm sorry," she said. "Now I must really go."

She leaned back in her seat, pushed the button to slide the window up, and the car slowly started moving forward again. I stood still, staring at the red taillights as they inched away.

Then the car stopped. I went running toward it, my heart in my throat. She had reconsidered. She had maybe seen my beautifully put-together outfit and realized that there was something more to me after all. She was going to hire me!

The window came down again.

"What was your name?" she asked.

"Indie," I said, a smidgen of hope returning. She remembered me after all!

"Look, Indie. I don't know about that internship. But maybe there is another way you can help me."

I stood still and silent, perplexed.

"Where are you from, anyway?" she asked.

"Here," I replied. "I mean, I'm Indian. My parents are from Calcutta. But I was born here."

"Do you have any experience with children?" she asked.

"I have an eight-year-old brother," I replied, confused by the question. "Why?"

Aaralyn paused for a second.

"I hear that people from your part of the world are good with domestic duties," she said, glancing at a lilac-painted fingernail. "I have a kid. He's two. I'm desperate for a weekend babysitter. I can't seem to find anybody who's interested in giving up their Saturday afternoon to hang out with a baby. If you're interested . . ."

I couldn't imagine Aaralyn Taylor with a child. She had never mentioned him in any of the interviews I'd read about her or in the weekly editorial she wrote in her magazine. I couldn't imagine her hugging a baby and changing diapers and kissing and cooing. There had never been mention of a husband either, if indeed there was one. Aaralyn didn't seem like the kind of woman who would ever iron anything or whip up scrambled eggs for the family on a lazy Sunday morning.

"I'll do it," I said, the words out of my mouth before I even had a chance to think about what I was saying. "But, um, don't you need to check references or anything?"

She cast a quick eye up and down me before scribbling down her home address and phone number.

"Saturday, ten A.M. Here," she said, handing me her name card. "No. Don't need references. You look pretty harmless to me. I'll pay you seven dollars an hour. Keep the whole day clear because I don't know how long I'll need you."

five

It wasn't until the limo had finally made its way through the gate, down the street, and out of sight that I finally turned around again and headed back toward the school building, stooping to pick up the bag that I had let fall from my shoulder. I was clutching on to Aaralyn Taylor's card like it was a lifeline, as if letting it out of my hand for even a second would mean that I would lose it forever.

Ahead, parked right outside the building, was my mother's dark green Hyundai. She was facing me, a book in her hand, her eyes planted firmly on me. She opened the door, stepped out of the car, and stood up, a woolen shawl draped over her short-sleeved T-shirt, gray socks on her sandal-clad feet.

"Can I ask what you are doing?" Her voice was stern, sterner than it had been in a long time. I was, for the most part, what would be considered a "good girl," so there was really rarely any reason for my parents to take any kind of tone with me. But now, she didn't look pleased.

"What are you doing running after somebody's car, dropping your bag on the ground? What was the urgency?"

I got into the front passenger seat, buckled up, turned on the radio, and tuned it to KISS-FM. "Fergalicious" was playing, and I tapped my foot in rhythm.

"Mom, you're not going to believe what just happened."

"Babysitting?" my father exclaimed. "You're getting the best education, you excel at your studies, and now you're going to do babysitting? Indira, what has come over you?"

As I had expected, my father was not impressed. His last patient of the afternoon had canceled, so he was home early. He had wanted to relax, to read the papers, and munch on some *chevda*—a spicy, crunchy trail mix—and maybe watch some CNN. But my mother had wasted no time in telling him that this coming Saturday, when I should be going to the Hindu temple with them and my younger brother, I was planning instead on spending the day at a strange woman's house, cleaning up after her child.

"Let alone the fact that you have never done any babysitting," my father chastised, reaching into the bowl. "You have never expressed an interest in such things. You don't even help out with your own brother as much as you should."

I turned to look at Dinesh, who was camped out in a corner with his LEGO pirate ship.

"Yeah," my brother said, his face impish. His teeth had wide spaces between them—my parents would be paying off a future orthodontist for the next decade—and his hair stuck up in all the wrong places. He was scrawny and mouthy and could be a real pest sometimes. But he called me *Didi*—big sister in Hindi—and I loved that.

"You can't look after a baby," he said. "Didn't you drop me on my head once?"

I ignored him, and turned back to my father.

"Dad, you know I'm really responsible. And it's not like it's a brand-new baby or anything. The kid is two. They just need someone to hang out with him, make sure he doesn't fall out of a window or anything. I'll be earning some extra pocket money. Haven't you been telling me I need to do that? Really, how hard can it be?"

All the way to Aaralyn Taylor's house the following Saturday morning, my father lectured me about what he described as my "poorly considered decision." I nodded politely as he spoke, but was far more preoccupied with how I looked. I had agonized for hours the night before over my attire for my first babysitting gig. I needed to be comfortable and not care if ketchup ended up on my clothes. But I had also ruled out sweatpants and sneakers, reminding myself that, baby or no baby, I was still going to Aaralyn Taylor's house. So I had opted for black capri-length jeans with a cute trim, thong sandals, and an old Aerosmith T-shirt I had found at a garage sale, which my parents couldn't believe I had spent eight dollars on, because it was somebody else's junk. I had slid on the mirrored bangles again and, around my neck, a carved bone pendant in the shape of the Om symbol. Stuffed into my bag was a floppy straw hat, the kind an American grandmother might once have worn but that was now instantly hot after Mischa Barton was spotted in one while vacationing in Hawaii. I had thrust it in at the last minute, hoping that perhaps this babysitting thing might entail a visit to the beach. While we were barely in the first flush of spring, the weather had been gorgeous recently, and Kim and I had the hit Santa Monica Pier the past two weekends.

The traffic was light on this sunny Saturday morning, and we whizzed along the freeway. I glanced at Aaralyn's name card and then at the directions that I had downloaded from MapQuest. Aaralyn lived in Brentwood, which I had only really heard about because Jennifer Garner and Ben Affleck lived there too. In fact, as far as I could recall, a lot of Hollywood stars made Brentwood their home. Aaralyn was probably even a next-door neighbor to a couple of them, saying hello as she stepped in and out of the limo that was inevitably always waiting outside her house, maybe carpooling with them to some glam event. I felt a chill go up my spine and a smile sneak across my face as I thought of all the sophisticated adventures that lay ahead of me.

I told my father that I would call him an hour before I was due to leave, to give him ample time to come and get me. He sighed, obviously considering that this little job of mine was going to cost him three hours of drive time today alone.

"I hope this is just a one-time thing," he said as we pulled up outside Aaralyn's house. I peered through the car window. In my mind, I had envisioned a grand mansion, the kind of place with security cameras all around it, a high gate topped with spikes, a circular courtyard with a fountain right at its center, a place like Madonna might live in.

But from the outside, the house looked smaller and a bit more ordinary than I had imagined, the only clues that someone successful lived here being the sparkling silver BMW convertible that was pulled up in the driveway.

I turned to wave good-bye to my father and slowly made my way up the path leading to the house, noticing plastic toys and a Radio Flyer Little Red Wagon on the lawn.

I rang the doorbell and heard the whirring of a vacuum cleaner gradually stop. The door opened, and in front of me was a small dark-haired woman in her fifties, wearing a maid's uniform.

"Yes, miss?" she asked.

"Oh, hello, I'm here to see Aaralyn Taylor. She's expecting me."

"Oh, you new babysitter?" she asked. "Good. You come in. Kyle is go crazy today."

In the background, I heard a high-pitched screech, and what sounded like Aaralyn's voice yelling out, "Stop it! Stop it now!"

"Everybody crazy today," the woman said, stepping aside to let me in.

I stood in the foyer and looked around. It was far more stylish inside than the exterior let on. It was the kind of place I might have seen featured on the pages of *Elle Decor*, all cool tones and chunky pillar candles. The shrieking in the background was the only thing to pierce the calm of the place.

I heard footsteps on the stairs behind me and turned around. In front of me was a handsome man holding a coffee mug, wearing a striped bathrobe, a big smile on his face.

"Hello, you must be the new girl. What's your name?"

"Indie," I replied, shaking his hand nervously.

"Hey. I'm Juno. Aaralyn's husband. She told me a bit about you. Said you ran after her begging for the internship when she was leaving your school the other day? That's pretty enterprising, I'd say."

It sounded pathetic, the way he put it. Suddenly, I was embarrassed.

"Is she around? And the baby?" I asked, dying to change the subject.

"Don't tell me you can't hear them," he laughed. "Kyle's been acting up today. Terrible twos. And trust me, they're *really* terrible. And Aaralyn's stressing out about it, so it's been high drama since six this morning. But listen," he said, turning his ear toward an upstairs room. "It's quiet now. Come on, let's go upstairs so you can meet the little guy."

I still couldn't believe I was in Aaralyn Taylor's house, stepping on her carpet, looking at the family pictures that lined the wall as we walked upstairs. It was absolutely thrilling.

A door was left slightly ajar, the sound of a hair dryer coming from the other side. Juno knocked gently, but obviously Aaralyn couldn't hear anything. We walked in and I almost fainted in shock at what I saw. Aaralyn was sitting at a dressing table, a round brush in one hand and a hair dryer in another. Across her lay a red-haired boy whose face I couldn't see because it was buried in his mother's chest. Sophisticated, remote, inaccessible, worldly Aaralyn Taylor was breastfeeding a toddler, like they did in Africa or Thailand. Would wonders never cease?

"Best way to shut them up," she said as if reading my thoughts. She was still fussing with her hair although she had now turned the hair dryer off. She was looking straight into the mirror instead of at me and talking in a low, modulated voice. It sounded like it could have been her professional voice, the one she reserved for assistants and secretaries and drivers; it was cold and almost unfriendly. Juno was leaning against the frame of the door, listening to her, his face relaxed and open compared to her tense one.

"Our weekday nanny is great, even if she's"—at this point Juno lowered his voice—"illegal," he said. "But for the occasional weekend, I swear we've gone through every babysitter in the greater Los Angeles area. Hey, honey, remember that woman Patti?" he asked his wife, who nodded silently. "We thought she was a godsend," he said to me. "Until she mentioned that she had just seen her *parole officer*." He began chuckling. "Oh, and what about that girl Yvette?" Juno continued. "Remember how she wanted to feed Kyle black beans out of a can while watching Spanish soap operas?"

"And my favorite mistake would have to be Flora," Aaralyn added. I appreciated the fact that they were trying to make me comfortable by telling me all this, although it oddly made me more nervous. I had barely begun, and they were already comparing me to all the other babysitters that had let them down. "She lived in. A lady from the Philippines. She couldn't drive and was always asking us to run her errands for us. *"Ma'am, can you buy me pork so I can make adobo? Ma'am, can you take this to the post office? Ma'am, can you get me Ruffles potato chips, unsalted."* Aaralyn had lapsed into some weird hybrid accent, which made Juno laugh. It was obviously an unguarded moment, something to be shared just with her husband, because as soon as she realized that I was there and listening, she straightened up and her tone changed. It was almost as if she didn't want me to see that side of her.

"So, as you can see, we've had our share of bad luck with babysitters," she said to me now, composing herself. "And, of course, the second we find somebody decent, Kyle doesn't like them. I've used several agencies, put ads in papers, asked friends of friends. I've even attempted poaching other peoples' nannies—parks are great places for that. I see someone who looks wonderful and immediately get a case of nanny envy. But nothing has ever worked out longer than a day or two. That's why we're always looking for somebody new."

She picked up a canister of hair spray, one of at least a dozen that sat on the counter in front of her.

"But truth be told, I didn't think you would show up. It's always the young girls who bail, especially on a Saturday. Something more interesting always turns up."

"I'm not like that," I said, looking down on the ground. Kyle had broken away from his mother's chest, leaving her exposed. I suddenly felt like I was invading a special mother-son moment, although the fact that

Aaralyn Taylor was doing her hair at the same time somehow made it less momentous. "When I say I will do something, I do it."

"Good attitude," she said, actually looking away from her hair and at me.

She finally put down her hairdressing tools, grabbed her sleeping son, and carried him to the bed. Juno turned around and left the room. She put Kyle down, covered him with a blanket, and kissed him softly on the forehead. Maybe she was a good mother after all.

"This is about the only time I can handle this motherhood thing," she said. "When he's sleeping. The rest of the time it's just one annoyance after another."

I looked down at him. His hair was soft and curly and framed an angelic face. He had healthy pink cheeks, fair skin, full lips, and a slightly upturned nose that was definitely inherited from his mother. At first sight, he reminded me of a cherub in a Renaissance painting.

"He's lovely," I said.

"Thank you," Aaralyn answered, looking at her son. "We're lucky, I guess. With babies, you never know what you're going to get. Anyway, back to business," she continued, her voice taking on that officious tone again. "Juno and I will be leaving shortly. We'll be gone most of the day. But Blanca, my housekeeper, will show you where everything is."

"Wait!" I shouted. The horror of it all had finally hit

home. I had never been alone with a two-year-old that belonged to someone outside of my family. What if something happened? These people had lawyers. They could sue. My dad was right. What was I thinking?

"I thought I would just be hanging out here with him, but that you would be here too," I said, realizing I was sounding stupid.

"Then what would I need you for?" Aaralyn asked icily. "Look, I've checked you out. I'm not that naive that I would let a total stranger into my house. After I got home the evening of the talk at your school, I called my niece, Brooke. She said you were nice and reliable."

Nice and reliable. The most popular and cosmopolitan girl in school had barely even noticed me, and now the only thing she could describe me as was nice and reliable. Like a German shepherd.

"You'll be fine," Aaralyn said, standing up and throwing on a Marni coat before dabbing on some perfume. She patted me on the shoulder and walked out the door. "Kyle can be a dream. Really."

I prayed that he would sleep for hours, leaving me to roam around Aaralyn's house. I switched on the baby monitor and went back downstairs, where Blanca, the maid, was in the kitchen preparing a pot roast.

"You drink something?" she asked, motioning to a cooler with a see-through door, filled with diet soda and bottles of Naked juice. I helped myself to a bottle of tangerine juice and went back into the living room. Blanca took it upon herself to show me around.

"All this, not for baby," she said, motioning to the immaculate living room and attached dining area, which featured a chandelier that hung almost to the table, and high-backed chairs covered in beige satin. "Baby only here," she continued, pointing to the kitchen.

It was probably normal in these circles to have "baby-free" zones. I thought back to my own upbringing, where the entire house was one big playpen, as far as Dinesh and I were concerned. To this day, my father would remind me of how many times he had stepped on tiny Matchbox cars and heads of dolls that I'd pulled off. My mother would cover the couch with an old bedsheet, and the carpets with a tarp, and we would be allowed to paint and sketch and roll and giggle wherever we wanted. My father had a small office at home, converted from a bedroom off the den, and even when he was in there, going over reports or researching some obscure medical condition, his door was always open to us. As a consequence, we learned to respect where we were and knew instinctively what we could touch. Our home was never zoned for attention and love.

"And baby never go there," said Blanca, pointing to a room off the foyer. I peered inside: It was a home office, an L-shaped desk against one wall holding an Apple G5 computer. Above it was a degree made out to Juno Taylor from a college of naturopathy, and next to it a host of other diplomas and certificates in things I'd never heard of like Native American ethnobotany and iridology. No wonder Aaralyn seemed so high-strung; her husband probably never allowed her to take any Prozac.

"Sir, he some kinda doctor," she said, noticing me reading Juno's certificates. "Has clinic behind house." She pointed through the window toward what looked like a guesthouse or artist's studio in the back, beside a large oak tree.

Despite the wall mountings, it was clear that this was Aaralyn's space. The surface of the desk was covered with previous issues of *Celebrity Style*. A mound of press kits was stacked in one corner, and Post-it notes were everywhere. There were framed photographs of Aaralyn with people I had long admired from afar: Oscar de la Renta on one side and Jennifer Aniston on the other, Selma Blair and Miuccia Prada, Charlize Theron and Michael Kors: the best people in fashion and the biggest stars in Hollywood.

On a notepad were what looked like story ideas for the next several issues: "The Style Evolution of Rosario Dawson," "Jessica (Simpson) vs Jessica (Alba): The Fashion Face-off," "Is Black Back?" Just staring at those words got me excited: I had never even stepped into a magazine office before, but I could already see how those stories would unfold, what pictures they would use, how they could be done with savvy. For a second, I forgot what I was really doing here in this house, so immersed was I in the world inside this office.

And then I heard the wailing through the monitor.

six

When I went back upstairs to get him, Kyle took one look at me, realized I wasn't his mother, and started screeching. No matter what I did, I couldn't calm him. I shushed in his ear, rocked him on my shoulder, tried to distract him with some crystal earrings I found dangling from an earring tree on Aaralyn's dressing table. But still he wailed. I reached for the monitor and turned it off, not wanting Blanca to hear the baby's distress. He squirmed out of my arms and tumbled back on the bed again, which caused him to cry even louder.

"Mama!" he screamed. "*Maaaaammmmaaaa!*"

I scooped him up and turned him to face outward so he couldn't push against me. I decided to head toward his room, which was down the corridor and across the hallway and seemed as good a place to go as any. Then Blanca showed up with a sippy cup and a plate of sliced bananas. I was relieved to see her, until I realized that she was only there to deliver the food, and was going back down to resume her cooking.

"What do I do with him?" I asked, his face turning red as he continued to scream.

"You give him food, change diaper. Maybe then he be better," she said loudly, trying to make herself heard above the din.

I found a bib folded on a table, and wrapped it around Kyle's neck. I handed him the sippy cup and he threw it across the room where it hit a wall, cracking the lid open and leaving a streak of orange juice on the pale blue carpet.

"Great," I said under my breath as I reached for a box of wet wipes nearby to try and clean up the mess. In the meantime, Kyle had shoved his tiny pudgy fingers into the bananas and began smearing them down his shirt and in his hair. He stopped crying when he realized how much fun he was having, giggling instead.

"Blanca!" I called out. "Help!"

She came back upstairs, saw Kyle with a face full of banana and the stain of juice on the floor, and began laughing.

"You no do this before, yes?" she asked. "You no babysitter?"

I realized that I was in over my head. There had to be an easier way to get close to Aaralyn Taylor.

"Come. Your first day, I help you," said Blanca,

scooping up the child while I followed them meekly, feeling like a child myself. We headed into his bathroom, which was decorated with yellow duckling decals all over the walls, took off his clothes, and immersed him in a lavender-scented bubble bath. He frolicked in the tub, squirting water out of a red plastic dolphin, while I played peekaboo with the duckling-emblazoned shower curtain. Finally, he was happy.

Cleaned and bathed, the bits of banana shampooed out of his hair, Kyle's mood was drastically improved. Blanca served us lunch—mashed potatoes, a boiled egg, and sliced steamed carrots for him, all oddly drowning in ketchup, and a turkey sandwich for me. When he refused to eat, I did the old airplane trick, the one I had seen my mom do on Dinesh, where I pretended the spoon of food was an airplane swooping down, needing a place to touch down.

"It's going to land in your mouth!" I said as Kyle opened up wide, swallowed his food, and then squealed in delight. His plate finally clean, we went back upstairs to play. Both of us crouching on the floor, we rolled a small rubber ball around, his face brightening in delight every time he caught it between his pudgy hands. I pulled funny faces, causing him to shriek with laughter, which ended up making *me* laugh. This babysitting thing was a cinch after all.

I pulled out several tubs of paint and a few brushes from a box, Kyle clapping his hands when he saw what we were going to do next. Outside the room on the carpeted hallway was a small stack of newspapers stretching back a few days, so I brought some in and laid them down. I couldn't find any plain paper, so I helped Kyle paint on the printed words of the *Los Angeles Times*, his little brush sweeping over headlines and photographs.

Then I heard my cell phone ring in my purse and raced downstairs to get it, figuring it was probably my dad wondering what time to come and fetch me.

It was Kim, calling to find out how my day was going.

"Not bad so far," I said, leaning up against a wall. "This house is beautiful, and oh my God, I even saw Aaralyn's office where she had all these photographs of her with celebrities and fashion designers. She's even more glamorous than I thought! It really put it all in pers—"

Just then, I heard a key in the door. Juno and Aaralyn were standing right in front of me.

"What are you doing down here?" she asked. "Where's my child?"

At that moment, a piercing wail came from upstairs.

"Crap," I said under my breath, hanging up the phone without saying good-bye to Kim.

The three of us, followed by Blanca, raced back up the flight of steps and toward Kyle's room. He was squatting on the floor, bright blue paint around his mouth, red fingerprints all over the walls and, if that wasn't bad enough, overturned pots of yellow and green liquid in a basket of clean clothes.

"What on *earth* happened here?" Aaralyn screamed. Her face was as red as the paint on the wall, her eyes ablaze. "You left my child *alone?!* You left a toddler *alone*?! What were you *thinking?*"

Blanca had covered her face with her hands. I started to cry. Kyle, realizing that his parents were now in front of him, was now gurgling gleefully, spitting out paint.

"At least that stuff isn't toxic. I'm all about vegetable dyes," Juno said, grinning at me. "Look, let's just all calm down. No harm done, and no mess that a bit of Ajax won't take out. Right, Blanca?"

"Still, she left Kyle alone so she could talk on the phone!" Aaralyn yelled. "Blanca, pick Kyle up and clean him off. I don't want him getting paint all over my clothes."

"Honey, calm down," Juno said, stroking his wife's back. Then his eyes fell upon the old newspapers spread out on the floor.

"Where did you get those?" he asked, now frowning.

"I found them outside, in the corridor," I stammered.

"Jesus," he said softly. "I was saving those. There were some important things in there I needed to clip. I wish you had checked with me first."

I cried even more. I wasn't even thinking about the intern job anymore. I had messed this up royally.

"I think you'd better call your parents and have them come and pick you up," Aaralyn said, her voice frosty. "You can wait downstairs until they get here. We'll take care of Kyle now."

Sheepishly, I went back downstairs to use my cell phone. I called my dad, who told me he had decided to visit some friends of his not too far from where I was, and said he would be there in fifteen minutes. He could obviously hear the distress in my voice, because he immediately asked me what was wrong. I whispered that it was nothing, but I just wanted to leave.

I picked up my bag, and told Aaralyn and Juno that I would wait outside. Aaralyn reached into a drawer and pulled out some money.

"Oh please, no," I said, holding up my hands. "I can't take that. I did a terrible job. I'm really sorry about everything."

Just then, Blanca came back downstairs with a cleaned up and happy Kyle. She put him down on the floor and he toddled toward me.

"Bye-bye," I said, smiling for the first time in the past twenty minutes.

He grabbed my pant leg and suddenly started crying.

"No go," he said through tears. "You no go."

A look of surprise crossed Aaralyn's face.

"Well, *that's* a first," she said, glancing over at her husband. "Usually, Kyle could care less."

"Maybe we should listen to him then," Juno said, looking at me sympathetically. "She seems like a sweet girl. And it wasn't her fault about the newspapers—I probably shouldn't have left them lying around. Maybe our son has good instincts."

"She doesn't have enough experience," Aaralyn said, talking about me as if I wasn't there. "Kyle might like her, but I just won't have peace of mind leaving him with her again." She looked at me again. My body was hot and tingling. I felt small and stupid.

Then I heard the honk of my father's car outside.

seven

I was so miserable I wanted to stay home, to cry on the phone with Kim while moping around in my favorite pink drawstring pants with the big red hearts printed on them. Despite the sunshine earlier today, the late afternoon had turned overcast and soggy. I wanted to drown my sorrows in a chocolate milk shake covered in a froth of whipped cream. For tonight, I didn't want to think about calories. I just wanted to languish in bed like a fallen television starlet. And I knew that I could count on Kim to not just sympathize, but to be available to me. Unless she was out with her parents, she was *always* home on Saturday night. In that sense, she and I were very alike.

But my parents had included me in their plans without even asking me if I was interested. I hadn't told them how badly my day had gone, because I didn't want to see the smug grin that would no doubt emerge on my father's face, to hear the "I told you so's" that I knew were just waiting for me on the tip of his tongue. When he had asked me why I looked upset, I replied that I had had a hard time keeping Kyle happy because he didn't know me.

"Babies are like that," he said, oddly trying to comfort me. "You can't take it personally."

So I had had absolutely no excuse for not accompanying them tonight.

"It is your uncle's birthday and we are all going!" my father had said sternly, even though I started to protest and told him I was tired.

"And yes, my dear child, may I inquire what it is you have done today that has caused such fatigue to come over you?"

Whenever my father felt the need to be sarcastic, he would often lapse into the very formal English he learned at boarding school in Calcutta. After twenty years in America, he still wasn't able to shake that off.

"Dad, do you *have* to sound like a science professor from the 1800s?" I asked, realizing that unless I was careful, this would escalate into a real conflict. But my nerves were already frayed and I was counting the minutes till I could delve into that rich chocolate shake.

My father took a deep breath.

"You played with a small child for a few hours with the assistance of a housekeeper in a fancy house. Get a *real* job, and maybe then you can complain of fatigue! I have been operating on people's brains all week. Do you see me complaining? No!"

"Dad, Uncle Mohit isn't even my real uncle."

My father couldn't argue that point, but it didn't make a difference. I knew that all my dad's random friends had to be called "uncle" by my brother and me, whether they were related by blood or not. And I knew just what kind of a party it would be: all the men clustered around the bar, talking about low-interest rates and high property prices, and all the women in the living room, discussing Saif Ali Khan's latest film, and whether frozen *parathas* could ever be as good as the freshly made ones.

But I could see even at the outset of the disagreement that there was no getting out of tonight's engagement. We were going as a family, my father had intoned. My staying home was not part of the plan. I mentally kissed my milk shake good-bye and headed for the shower.

Fifteen minutes later, I was wrapped in a towel, my hair still dripping wet. I stood in front of my closet, its mirrored panels slid all the way back, gazing at my clothes, like I always did before I was getting ready to go anywhere.

"Don't wear those trendy-bendy-type clothes," my mother said, stopping briefly as she walked past my room. "Last time we met with Uncle and Aunty they wondered why you had on a hat the whole time and that long long scarf that went past your knees. Remember, they were asking you if you had just returned from a trip to Antarctica?" she laughed.

"Don't worry, Mom," I said, rolling my eyes. "Long scarves are so last season anyway."

I looked back at the racks and shelves of clothes, and moaned under my breath about having nothing to wear. My favorite tweed pleated skirt was at the dry cleaner's, although my mother especially hated that one, complaining that I looked like a convent school student. She also disliked my cargo pants, wondering each time I wore them why I needed that many pockets in anything, and was horrified at my distressed and whiskered denim jacket, convinced that I looked like I was homeless.

"Wear something Indian," she insisted, calling out from her room. "Tunic, pants, *dupatta*. So easy. No fuss-muss."

I sighed. I had plenty of those, but hated wearing them on their own, always preferring to team a long silk *salwar* top with a pair of faded jeans, or my *churidar* pants with a soft layered T-shirt. My mother always thought I was a bit disrespectful when I dressed like that, telling me that I was diluting the beauty of our native garb and, consequently, the purity of our culture.

"This is not how your grandmothers would dress," she would say to me.

"Mom, that's kinda the point," I would say back.

But tonight, I gave in. I pulled out a claret-colored silk top that came down to my knees, and which was printed with tiny gold flecks. It came with matching pants and a soft chiffon scarf that wound around my neck. From a box in a drawer I took out matching glass bangles and a *bindi*, and slipped into beige *kohlapuri* sandals. I looked in the mirror, and let out a "yecch."

"Mom, I look like a village bride!" I yelled out.

"Nothing wrong in that," she yelled back, not even bothering to come and see for herself. "It is just for one night."

I turned to gaze at myself in the mirror again and wondered what Aaralyn Taylor would do—reminding myself that I would never find out because she wanted to have nothing to do with me ever again. I imagined her talking to the next babysitter the way she had talked to me this morning, ridiculing all the girls who had come before, and then mentioning me as another example of someone who could do nothing right. I would be the totally inept one, the one who left her child alone long enough for him to do serious damage to his nursery.

I cocked my head to one side and pulled the scarf off my neck, replacing it with a chunky choker. I kicked off my boring sandals and found a pair of fake snakeskin high-heeled pumps I had picked up on sale at the mall the previous week. I turned up the cuffs of my long-sleeved top, and removed the set of glass bangles, replacing it with a thick red-strapped watch instead. I ran a dollop of gel through my hair. Then I stepped back and took another look.

Much better, I thought to myself.

. . .

Uncle Mohit's house was not far from ours. He and his wife, Meena, lived with their three daughters in a colonial house in a gated community less than fifteen minutes away. They were prominent members of what my father kept referring to as "the community," meaning that they were very good about attending religious festivals at the temple, arranging fund-raisers whenever some calamity hit the subcontinent, and generally being a great source of information on anything and everything that affected Indians in the Valley. Like my father, Uncle Mohit was a doctor, although he worked in emergency medicine at a nearby hospital. He and his wife had had their daughters just a year apart and had given them cutesy names that might have been fun if they had been born in Mumbai a couple of decades ago, but were just too silly for words in modern Los Angeles. Rinky was sixteen, Pinky was seventeen, and Tinky was eighteen, and they were, without a doubt, among the most annoying girls I had ever met.

When we walked in, I forced a smile as the trio of "inkys" stepped forward to kiss me on the cheek. They were all in Indian outfits too, but worn in the traditional way, and all in similar shades of green. Long golden earrings dangled from their pretty earlobes.

"How *are* you?" Pinky asked, staring at my spiky, shiny hair, while her older sister gazed down at my python shoes.

"Interesting outfit," Rinky chimed in, a ring of sarcasm in her voice.

This was going to be a long night.

I stepped into the living room, and, as I predicted, saw a sea of women dressed in saris or tunic-pants outfits like mine—worn conventionally—helping themselves to freshly fried *pakodas* and plates of *bhel*. My father had already made his way into an adjacent room, which had been converted into a bar, and my brother had disappeared upstairs, where some of the other boys his age were experimenting with someone's Nintendo Wii.

My mother squeezed into a small space on the sofa next to Aunt Meena, and I hoisted myself onto the armrest next to her. I had been here only five minutes, but was already mind-numbingly bored. From what I could gather, there didn't seem to be anybody here for me to talk to. The only people here my age were the "inkys," and, well, enough said.

The "inkys" came into the living room, smiling and holding plates of spicy appetizers and paper napkins to pass around. I looked at them, recalling my father's always-complimentary remarks about them. He boasted about their abilities as if they were his own daughters— their straight A's, their skill at *Bharatanatyam* dancing, the fact that they could sing the latest crop of Hindi film songs as well as something from forty years ago. They only watched Zee TV, which covered news and music from India, and had never even switched channels to the CW. My parents, for all their mostly modern outlook on life, thought that I should be more like the "inkys," closer to "the community" and less involved in what they often described as "American nonsense." The "inkys," they would often remind me, could read, write, and speak fluent Hindi, had learned all the lyrics to *Om Jai Jagdish*, the devotional song that many religious Hindus sang every morning, and knew how to perfectly work a pressure cooker. The only way I could ever make *dal* was if I microwaved it right in the packet.

As dinner was being served, Rinky found me, even though I attempted to hide behind my mother.

"So, what are your plans for the summer?" she asked, though we just finished spring break. "Will you be looking for a job somewhere?"

"I hope to," I replied, having learned from experience to keep my conversations with these girls as brief as possible, knowing that they interpreted things in the weirdest way and told their parents everything.

"Yes, Pinky and Tinky and I have already lined things up," she said, laying down a big platter filled with steaming *biryani*. "The three of us are returning to India for a couple of months, and will divide our time between yoga workshops in Karnataka, working with Mother Teresa's missions in Calcutta, and assisting with a charity in Delhi that is still raising money for the tsunami victims. Still such suffering after all this time. Can you believe it?" she asked, tut-tutting quietly. "Hey, Indie, maybe you should come with us!" she said, her eyes suddenly brightening. "You'll *love* it! It's *so* fulfilling!"

Rinky was right. What she and her sisters planned to do over the summer sounded selfless and charitable and would probably help no end of people and catapult the three of them to the front of the line when the time came for them to get into heaven. And I had to confess to feeling a little envious of their planning and foresight; that in a few months, they'd be off trying to change the world, while I would still be smarting at the knowledge that I'd failed miserably at looking after a toddler.

Rinky looked up at me, a pair of plastic tongs in one hand, waiting for some kind of response.

"Thanks for asking, Rinks," I said, using the pet name that her parents always called her by. "But I don't think I'll be able to make it." I wished I had that internship at *Celebrity Style* to tell them about, something to wipe off that supercilious look they all seemed to share.

"Really?" Rinky said. "What will you be doing?"

"Well, I really can't say," I said, my face suddenly turning warm. "I'm waiting for everything to be confirmed."

"Must be your fashion thing, right?" Rinky asked. "You're always going on about it. We find it all very superficial ourselves, but if *that's* how you want to waste away your life, feel free."

I clenched my fists tight at my side.

"Actually, it's a wonderful internship, interviewing movie stars and famous fashion designers," I blurted out. "It's a top magazine, but if you've only ever read your mummy's Indian magazines, then you've probably never even heard of it. But some people think it's even better than *Vogue*, you know. The editor liked me so much that I've already started. I had my first day today." I told myself that I wasn't so much lying as embellishing the truth a little. The editor did like me—or at least had until the fiasco earlier today. And I supposed that if everything had gone according to plan, and I was living in some parallel universe, I *would* be interviewing movie stars and famous fashion designers, right?

My father, in the meantime, had suddenly appeared behind me. I detected a whiff of whisky on his breath. My father rarely drank alcohol, waiting only until loud social events like this one to indulge in a glass or two of Johnnie Walker. It always made him merry and chatty.

"Ah, Indie, having a good time?" he asked, slapping me on the back with one hand and reaching out for a plate with another. "I see you're talking to the lovely Rinky here. Such smart smart girls, all of them," he said as Rinky smiled politely.

"So, what do we have here?" he asked, glancing at the table. "Such a feast! Rice, vegetables, lamb, chicken, shrimp—my my, you girls have really gone all out," he said, his speech now sounding a little slurred. Was my father actually tipsy?

My father was usually the soul of discretion, a firm believer in thinking before speaking and generally speaking as little as possible. But now, it was as if someone had given him the gift of the gab—and it was nonreturnable.

"I'm just *ravenous!*" he said. "This daughter of mine kept me out of the house for hours today, driving her back and forth to her new job." I prayed that my father would stop right there. He had said just enough to give me a little respect in the eyes of the "inkys."

But Johnnie Walker obviously had a mind of his own.

"Yes, babysitting," he said, using a large wooden fork to pull out vegetables from a salad bowl. "In our day, no girl would ever consider babysitting as a job. But our Indie here, that seems to be how she wants to spend her time. She came home today with dried paint and pee-pee stains all over her clothes!" And with that, my father let out a big, inebriated guffaw and moved on.

I wanted the roof to cave in. I wanted there to be an earthquake that was at least a six on the Richter scale, something that would cause these three sisters to forget everything they had just heard.

But the earth stayed intact, the party carried on, and Rinky broke out into giggles, gathering her sisters close and telling them what she had just heard.

"Not that there's anything wrong with that," Pinky said, her expression turning even more patronizing than it usually was. "But couldn't you have found anything else? Gosh, we had *no* trouble getting ourselves organized, did we?" she said, turning back to her sisters.

"I was just helping out my boss today," I said, refusing to let the irritating "inkys" get the last word in.

I grabbed a plate, piled on some food, and stomped out to the patio where I found a quiet seat. I glanced over at the "inkys," who were being the most perfect and gracious hostesses, chatting amiably with all their guests.

After my dismal babysitting debut this morning, part of me had just given up. No matter what I had said to the "inkys" just now, my confidence had actually sunk to a new low. Was it only a few weeks ago that I had typed out what was nothing less than an ode to fashion, that I came up with exactly 200 perfectly crafted words for the internship application essay?

But sitting here now, looking at their collective charm and self-assurance, something in me shifted. I closed my eyes and thought for a moment about what my mother would do if she were in that situation, how she would come out of it.

The other girls in my class had mothers who were their friends. They shared clothes, went shopping together, lunched afterward, and talked about boys.

My mother was not one of those mothers. She had

arrived in America from India as a shy bride, and had worn simple cotton saris until I was three years old, when her *pallav* had gotten caught beneath the base of a merry-go-round at a local street carnival, and she had then decided that she couldn't possibly be an effective mother if she was constantly worrying about six yards of fabric on her body. So she had packed up all the saris gifted to her by her parents as part of her trousseau, stashed them in the attic, and had gone to Kmart to stock up on classic-cut jeans and oversized T-shirts, which had remained her signature look ever since. Her hair was almost always tied in a ponytail, she wore nothing on her face except for a tiny slather of Pond's skin cream, and she virtually lived in simple, comfortable leather slippers. She took me to Little League matches and Girl Scout bake sales dressed in the same nondescript way, always nodding courteously to the other moms as they sashayed past in slim sweatpants, tight hoodies, and big tortoiseshell sunglasses. My mother would always comment that the other mothers and daughters could be big sister and little, and my friends' moms would smile, unable to truthfully return the compliment.

It wasn't that my mother was that much older than me. She was only twenty-three when I was born, her face still pretty and unlined and dewy now at thirty-eight. But unlike the other moms who attended thrice-weekly Pilates classes and had meals from The Zone delivered to their doors, my mother enjoyed being fleshy and full, seeing no need to eliminate white rice, ghee, and thick buttermilk curries from her diet. She was the quintessential homemaker, the plain and sturdy and kindhearted sort you might otherwise see as the subject of a makeover on *The Tyra Banks Show*, if she had ever been so inclined. I sometimes wished that she would take more of an interest in how she dressed and in the clothes that hung in her closet. But every time I suggested to her that maybe we could go shopping, that maybe there could be more to her style than elastic-waist pants and three-quarter-sleeved cotton T-shirts, she would stare at me blankly and then put her glasses back on, the plain pair that would hang around her neck on a plastic cord.

Even though I had told neither one of my parents exactly what had happened, that didn't mean I couldn't be inspired by them nonetheless.

I looked over at my mother now, who was helping herself to dinner and chatting with her friends. With her poise and quiet dignity, she would always find a way to get back into the good graces of someone she had admired for so long. If she were me, she would call to apologize, perhaps send a token of her regret, would approach a difficult situation with humility and strength. She would not give up and she had not brought me up to give up either.

There was still time before the intern would be chosen. Somehow, I *had* to make amends.

eight

My cell rang at the ungodly-for-a-Sunday-morning hour of 8:30 A.M. I never understood what compelled Kim to get up that early when it wasn't a school day.

She had called to ask me how I was feeling. Truth be told, despite my newfound resolve from last night, in the cold, clear light of day I was now feeling depressed and defeated again. Keeping your spirits up is hard work. Maybe I'd feel better after some Ovaltine and toast, and could start plotting my next course of action.

"Don't you think you're being a little dramatic?" Kim asked when I told her I couldn't stop thinking about yesterday. "It's not the end of the world. It's just a job. There'll be others."

"*Just a job? Just a job?*" I repeated. "I really blew it, Kim. I know I need to figure out how to get back in the game, but that doesn't hide the fact that I still blew it."

My mother knocked on the door.

"What, Mom?" I said through the door.

"Phone call for you," she answered. "That Aaralyn lady."

I hung up on Kim once again and raced to the door. Just as I took the cordless out of my mother's hand, my mind went to the worst-case scenarios: Aaralyn might have discovered something else I'd done wrong and was going to tell me about it; maybe Kyle had to be hospitalized with dysentery this morning because of something I fed him yesterday. Maybe I'd cracked an expensive crystal vase without knowing it. Maybe Aaralyn just wanted to yell at me some more. So I don't know why I was so anxious to get to the phone: It couldn't have been good, whatever it was.

"Good morning, Indie, Aaralyn Taylor here," she said, her voice clipped and brisk, which must be quite an accomplishment for a Sunday morning.

"Listen, after you left yesterday, Kyle was inconsolable. He cried for a good thirty minutes, which was a complete chore for me to deal with. And he's been asking for you ever since he got up at six this morning. I swear, the child is an insomniac. He's been calling you 'dindy,' which is at once endearing and irritating." She spoke, barely taking a pause, but the words coming out of her mouth were like music to my ears. Kyle liked me! Sweet, messy, ketchup-addicted, little two-year-old Kyle liked me!

"I gather yesterday was your first time doing something like this," she said, finally inhaling. "So I'm prepared to overlook that rather shaky start and see if you'd like to try it again."

My heart did a little leap.

"Um, yes, I think I'd like that," I said, my voice trembling. "Again, I'm *so so* sorry about yesterday."

"It's okay. Let's move on," Aaralyn said abruptly. I could imagine her talking to Kyle like that every time he had a meltdown.

"I could probably use some help today. Can you come by?"

My father again complained all the way as he drove me over, accusing me of taking him away from some guy called Bob Schieffer who was on some really boring political show.

"TiVo it, Dad," I said as we buckled ourselves into the car.

"TiVo is not a verb, Indira," he replied.

"Indie," I corrected him.

Juno let me in when I got there, telling me that Aaralyn was on the phone in her office. Kyle was playing on an alphabet mat on the floor in the kitchen, building a tall tower out of soft blocks, and then knocking it over.

"Italy," Juno said, sitting me down and motioning to Aaralyn's office. "She's been on the phone for thirty minutes. Although what *they're* doing working on a Sunday evening I'll never understand. I thought Italians relished their weekends." He picked Kyle up and put him on my lap and began coaching me in the baby's various grunts and moans.

"Now, when it's a high-pitched wail and it comes from nowhere, it means he's tired and could use a little nap," said Juno. "But if it's a succession of whimpers, you could try giving him his pacifier or handing him a snack. If his mother is around, she could nurse him. But I can usually get him to do anything with a handful of animal crackers," he said, smiling. "Otherwise, just keep him entertained and he'll be fine."

I didn't dare hope that Juno was investing in me in some way, that he wouldn't take the time to explain these things to me if I was just a one- or two-time babysitter. I looked down at Kyle and suddenly felt a little guilty; his eyes were wide open and innocent, his little fists clutched, a smear of raspberry jam clung to his bottom lip. I realized then that he was really just a means to an end for me, that I wouldn't be here if I was hoping to achieve something else.

Aaralyn finally emerged from her office, said a quick hello to me, kissed her son on his forehead, and then gazed out the window. "You know, the weather is nice enough for us to go to the park," she said. "Indie, come along." It was more of a directive than it was an invitation. "I'm going to need your help. I have some calls to make while we're out and will need someone to keep an eye on Kyle."

It took me fifteen minutes to load the car—snacks, stroller (two types, in case he didn't like one), buckets and shovels for the sandbox, a big parasol to shield his fine features from the sun. I wanted to make sure everything was covered. This was my second chance, and I was determined not to blow it.

Juno had decided to stay home, saying he had some paperwork to take care of. That would leave Aaralyn and me alone, not counting the kid, with plenty of time to talk and get to know each other. It would be my first opportunity to wow her with my fashion insight in addition to my capable babysitting skills.

"In the back," she said to me as I first attempted to get into the passenger side next to her. "Keep Kyle entertained while I'm driving."

My heart sank, but I followed her instructions. Back there, I felt like another child. She got on the freeway and said she was headed to her favorite park, known for its shady trees and safe playground equipment. She was dressed in Sunday casual chic; white cotton shirt, trim beige jeans, matching Tod's loafers, a roomy leather bag to carry all the things that wouldn't fit in Kyle's knapsack. Her large Jackie O–style sunglasses were perched atop her head, simple pearls in her ears. She was, even dressed down, the most perfectly put-together person I had ever seen.

As we cruised along, I started to feel peckish, realizing I hadn't eaten since breakfast. Without drawing Aaralyn's attention to it, I rummaged in Kyle's knapsack for something to nibble on; there were tiny bags of raisins, edamame beans, baby carrots. Where were the Mini Oreos and multicolored Fruit Loops I had grown up with? What fun was raiding his snack bag if everything in there was *healthy*?

"There's a packet of crackers in there, but I'd rather you not give them to him until you exhaust everything else," Aaralyn instructed, obviously seeing me delving into his snack bag from her rearview mirror. "I'm trying to limit his carb intake. Childhood obesity, you know," she said. "Early eating habits dictate how you'll eat the rest of your life." She glanced at me again through the mirror, her gaze briefly flitting to my stomach area, which felt even more flabby than usual. In a bid to stave off boredom the night before, I had eaten a huge amount at Uncle Mohit's house, including twelve *gulab jamuns* for dessert. Deep-fried cottage-cheese balls soaked in sugary syrup do not a low-carb diet make. I had to loosen the string around the waist of my *churidar* pants after that. And this morning, Dinesh had commented that I was looking "jigglier" than usual.

"Is that even a word?" I had scowled back at him.

Now, something in Aaralyn's tone felt like she was making a little dig at me, as if she were wondering what my parents fed me when I was two. Perhaps they should have done the edamame thing, I thought, still feeling my abdomen straining against the waist of my jeans today.

I picked up some carrot sticks, handed one to Kyle and crunched away with him.

Minutes after we slid into the carpool lane on the freeway, we noticed cars backing up in front. Before long, our brisk pace had slowed down to a crawl, and the neighboring lanes weren't much better.

"It's pretty bad traffic for a Sunday," I offered lamely, just wanting to make conversation.

Aaralyn ignored me, swearing under her breath and turning on the radio. She fiddled with the buttons until she hit a local news station, listening for traffic updates.

"And a sig alert on the four-oh-five North where a four-car collision has brought everything to a standstill at Olympic," the announcer intoned.

"How friggin' inconsiderate!" Aaralyn shouted. "A bunch of people drive badly, and the rest of us have to suffer for it!"

Instantly her mood had turned from what had been a pretty sunny one earlier in the day to completely sullen. When Kyle started fussing in his seat, Aaralyn turned around and hissed at him, scaring me in the process. This was one frightening woman. I wondered how her cheerful and easygoing husband put up with her on a day-to-day basis.

After another twenty minutes of inching along at a creeping pace, Aaralyn swore out loud, seemingly unconcerned that her impressionable toddler was awake in the backseat.

"Screw this!" she exclaimed. "I'm getting off this goddamn freeway!"

She placed one manicured hand on the horn and held it down, letting all the world know that she had more right than them to move ahead, that they had to make way for her. Once out of the snarling traffic, she consulted her GPS system for the correct street.

"Is the park near here?" I asked.

"To hell with the park," she said. "I'm not in the mood now. We're going to the office. It's right around the corner."

I was elated. I silently thanked the Hindu gods for throwing a traffic jam in our way—the first time I had ever been grateful for a freeway mess.

All this time, I had only imagined the headquarters of *Celebrity Style*. In my mind, it looked exactly like the place where Ugly Betty worked, all white-and-glass modernity. I had always wanted to see it. And now, as Aaralyn sulked and Kyle fussed next to me, I couldn't wait till the moment I stepped into those offices, till I could actually see where my most favorite magazine in the whole world was put together.

Once Kyle realized there was not going to be a swing set in his future this morning, his whining turned into a droning and then an all-out wail. I rummaged in his diaper bag for his bottle, took the lid off the nipple, and shoved it in his mouth.

nine

The security guard looked up and smiled when we walked in through the double glass doors. Kyle was squirming in my arms, the diaper bag weighed down my shoulder.

"Miss Taylor, in on another gorgeous Sunday?" he said jovially. "Oh, and who do we have here?" he asked, looking at Kyle. "My, how he's grown since I last saw him! My boy has just turned four, and I have—"

"Have a nice day, Ron," Aaralyn said, cutting him off and walking purposefully toward the elevator.

We rode up eight floors, my excitement mounting by the second. Not even Kyle, who was beginning to whine again, could dilute my enthusiasm.

The doors opened and we stepped out into a spacious lobby and made a right. Another set of glass doors had the words CELEBRITY STYLE etched on the front. Aaralyn took out a small plastic card from her bag, swiped it into a little keypad at the side of the door, and then punched in some numbers. A buzzer sounded, the door clicked open. We were in.

A semicircular reception desk greeted us, the chair behind it empty. We continued past it to a large, open space, filled with desks and computers and phones and files, Post-it notes and magazine clippings pinned to flat-screen desktops. There were charts and calendars and address books spread out over the dozen or so desks. Even in the emptiness of a Sunday afternoon, the place had a frenzied, busy look about it that just thrilled me.

Along one wall were cabinets with pretty gift bags overflowing with beauty products and other goodies, tied in ribbons and couched in confetti. This must have been the "swag" that I often read about.

Kyle was kicking my stomach, letting me know that he wanted to be put down. I turned around to ask Aaralyn if this was okay, and found that she wasn't standing behind me anymore.

"This way," I heard her call from a hallway.

I yanked Kyle toward his mother's voice and realized that we were standing in her own personal office. It was huge, organized, not a sheaf of paper out of place. It was much like her office at home, although the one thing that struck me was that there wasn't a single photograph of her family anywhere—no pictures of Kyle with drool hanging off his chin, or of her and Juno on a family vacation, nothing to indicate that she had much of a life outside this office.

I put Kyle down and he waddled over to his mother, stooping to play with the tiny wheels under her high-backed leather chair.

"Get him out of here before he crushes his fingers," she said, not looking up at me, her eyes on her computer screen instead, her hand on the translucent white mouse. I reached for the kid, wondering how he was going to let me pick him up without releasing one of his gut-busting screams, when we heard a voice outside.

"Hello? Miss Taylor? Back again?"

A pretty girl was standing in the doorway.

"What are you doing in on a beautiful Sunday?" the girl asked. "I've got everything under control. Honest, go home." The girl's eyes fell on me and then on Kyle scrambling by my feet.

"Look how big he's gotten!" she said.

"Yes, he's a kid. They grow," Aaralyn said drily. "Meghan, why are *you* here?"

"Oh, admin stuff," she said. "Getting freelancers' invoices processed, itemizing expenses. The kind of things I never get around to doing during the week."

Aaralyn nodded, although it seemed to me that she hadn't really been paying attention.

"Indie, this is Meghan, my assistant," said Aaralyn. "This is Indie . . . the babysitter."

The title "babysitter" stung more than I'd expected. But I guess it was true.

"Nice to meet you," Meghan said, extending her hand.

"You too," I said enthusiastically. "How long have you been working here?"

I couldn't believe I was asking a question, trying to fraternize. In India, as I could recall from all the times we went to visit relatives there, the help *never* tried to make conversation with anybody other than the other help. Even in my own house here, the lady who came to clean every week would never ask my parents a question unless it related to where the extra toilet paper was stashed.

Meghan more or less ignored me, turning her attention back to her boss.

"Let me know if there's anything I can help you with," she said. "I'll be at my desk."

Aaralyn nodded without looking up. I was dying to ask her what she was gazing at on her computer screen, what fascinating features she was working on, or what kind of photographs she was checking out, deciding if they were worth putting in the magazine or not. But Aaralyn was deep in thought and certainly wouldn't want to answer the questions of some fashion-obsessed adolescent, so I held my tongue, instead trying to distract Kyle by turning him toward the window and showing him a helicopter as it whirred by. I could see Aaralyn's face reflected in the glass, her expression studious and almost cross.

We didn't leave for another two hours, Kyle alternating between having fun and whining, giggling and crying. I would play hide-and-seek with him and he would have a smile on his face one minute and then burst into tears the next. Each time he made any noise, Aaralyn looked up and told me to tell her son to be quiet, as if I had any say in how he felt. When the noise was getting too much for her, I scooped him up and took him down the carpeted hallway, as far as I could possibly get from her, so she wouldn't have to hear her son's distress. I racked my brain to think of ways to keep him engaged.

I thought back to when Dinesh was this age and I was ten, and there were plenty of times my mother left me with him while she took a quick shower or made an important phone call. There were some things that had delighted him: swinging him upside down while holding his legs (probably the time I dropped him on his head), or chasing him around the furniture. It wasn't a good idea to do anything with Kyle that would distract his mother, but the words "play quietly" somehow didn't apply to a toddler.

We went into the corridor again so I could walk Kyle up and down, carrying him and pointing out the framed magazine covers on the walls.

"And look, there's Scarlett Johansson!" I said to him in a cooing voice. "And isn't her dress pretty? Oh yes, it's so pretty! And look there—that's Jessica Biel! Look at those arms! They are toned! Yes! She's wearing red! Say red, Kyle! Say red!"

When I realized I was sounding like a lunatic and that Kyle had absolutely no interest in a starlet's wardrobe choices, I continued walking until I got to the end of the hallway. On a closed door was a name, JENNIFER MITCHUM, that I recognized; this was the lady in the Human Resources Department I had sent my internship application to! The door had glass panels on each side and I peered through, not sure about what I expected to see on the other side. Even though I knew that my application was probably not there on the surface of her pale gray desk, I was oddly comforted by the fact that Jennifer Mitchum existed, and here I was, standing right outside her office. Somehow, it made the whole process real to me.

Kyle began whining again, so I sat down against the wall, stretched my legs out, and rested him on my knees. Then, without really thinking about it, I began singing a Hindi song about a horse and carriage, bouncing Kyle up and down on my lap as I chanted "ghoda ghoda gadi" over and over again.

I didn't hear Aaralyn step into the hallway looking for us.

"What *are* you doing?" she asked, looking a little peeved.

"Oh, it's just a Hindi song my parents used to sing to

me and my kid brother," I explained. Kyle had started fussing, wanting me to start up again.

"Well, I'd appreciate it if you wouldn't do that," she replied. "He's very impressionable. I want his first language to be perfect English, not some gibberish. I'm done," she announced, reaching out for her child and giving me her bag to hold. "Let's get out of here."

Aaralyn didn't say a word all the way home. I wondered what I had done wrong, if she was still miffed about me singing to Kyle in a foreign language. Did she catch me peering into Jennifer Mitchum's office?

As soon as we arrived at the house, she stormed out of the car and up the driveway, leaving me to bring in her son, who had fallen asleep, and all his belongings. I laid Kyle down in his room upstairs, turned on the monitor, and went into the kitchen, from where I saw Aaralyn and her husband talking animatedly in the backyard.

I knew I shouldn't be eavesdropping, but I was helping myself to a glass of water, and the words carried across the air and through the window. I didn't get the whole conversation, but it had something to do with an upcoming issue, the cover story of which was the recent wedding of the hot young movie actress Gina Troy.

"Her people *promised* us the exclusive!" Aaralyn yelled. "We've already done the interview! We were the ones to break the news! And those people, they've done it again! I *hate* GossipAddict!"

My ears perked up at the mention of a particularly salacious website.

"Keep your voice down, Aaralyn," Juno said, sounding his reasonable self. "Come on back to the clinic and I'll give you some Bach Flower Remedies."

"I don't want your goddamn remedies!" she yelled. "What I need now is a good lawyer, not your feel-good crap!"

She turned around, came back in through the kitchen, and climbed upstairs, not even looking at me. Juno came in, glanced over at me with an embarrassed expression on his face, and trailed after his wife, reaching into his pocket for a stack of ten-dollar bills that he left on the kitchen table.

I took that as my cue to call my dad.

ten

When we got home, a white cardboard box containing pizza was sitting on the dining room table. I was ravenous, but pizza dripping with melted cheese was probably the last thing I needed; I remembered Aaralyn's sly look through the rearview mirror in her car when we were discussing eating habits. She probably never ate pizza.

But this was a Sunday night tradition in our house. My mother would often joke that on Sundays her "kitchen was closed." I guess even she needed a break. So apart from her brewing some tea in the morning, we usually had to fend for ourselves, food-wise. Sometimes it was Chinese, on other days it might be kebabs and pita bread from the local shawarma place. But it was almost always too rich, too salty, too fried.

I peered into the white box; my mother had left two slices of pizza for me, plus some garlic bread. While I knew I could go into the kitchen and fix myself a salad, the smell of pepperoni called to me. After all, I'd been really good that day, eating only some fruit this morning and then basically being on an Aaralyn-enforced starvation diet while I was babysitting. The woman kept absolutely no junk food in her house. I stared at the pizza for a minute longer, thought back to Aaralyn's slightly accusing and completely withering look, and then gazed down at my "jiggly bits."

Yes, I would be good today. No pizza.

After my hastily arranged salad, I went upstairs and logged onto the GossipAddict.com website. I had heard of it before today, but never had a chance to visit it. I knew how popular it was, though; it was always being cited as a source by those anchors on the entertainment news shows that I loved watching in the evening. But between keeping up with my weekly issues of *Celebrity Style*, glancing at my Daily Candy snippets, and occasionally checking out style.com, I barely had time to see what else was out there in cyberspace. Homework, unfortunately, tended to get in the way of that.

But once I went to GossipAddict.com, I was able to see what Aaralyn had been so upset about: There, as the lead story, and complete with exclusive pictures, was a full detailed story on Gina Troy's wedding to her leading man lover, Pascoe Donovan. These were pictures nobody had ever seen before—and *shouldn't* have seen until the next week's issue of *Celebrity Style*, judging by what I had overheard from Aaralyn's conversation with her husband. Just reading the words on my computer and remembering the exchange earlier today sent a chill up my spine. It excited me no end to be close to such drama.

I went back downstairs and joined my parents in the den. A commercial was on in the middle of *Desperate Housewives*. My father turned to speak to me; somehow our family managed to have entire conversations while ads for cars and beer rolled on unheeded in front of us.

"So, what are your plans for all this?" he asked.

"Dad?"

"What is all this for? What is the final objective?" my father repeated. "By doing this babysitting, what are you hoping to achieve?"

It was a reasonable question, and one that I wished I could have easily answered.

After all, I did have a plan: to make myself so invaluable to Aaralyn and her family that she would find a place for me at her magazine.

I knew that confessing this to my dad would make me sound hopelessly naive. But I decided that I should tell him the truth.

"Well, Dad, I actually did have a plan," I said thoughtfully. "You know how much I love fashion and how I've always been interested in fashion journalism, right? You know that there's never been anything else I've ever wanted to do?"

He said nothing and just stared back at me.

"Aaralyn Taylor, the woman whose son I babysit—I really love her magazine. And there's possibly an internship available there this summer, and I *really, really* want it. More than anything. But lots of people want it. So when she asked me to help look after her child on weekends, I figured it would, you know, get me closer to her. That maybe she would see what I'm really all about, and would offer me the job. There's really nothing wrong with babysitting. It is a perfectly respectable thing to do. You know, Julia Roberts wished her nanny a happy birthday on television, at the Oscars. We provide a valuable service."

Even I had to concede that I sounded ridiculous at that point, comparing myself to the probably very experienced and competent nanny of a twenty million-dollar-a-movie film star.

My father sighed deeply, lifted himself out of the armchair he had been sitting in for the past two hours, and came toward me, easing down onto the couch next to me.

"Indie, my dear, what are we to do with you?"

He looked at me like I was five again, like I had never really grown up.

"Do you really think you have a chance?" he asked softly. "Do you really think that she would choose you, when there is no end to the more qualified girls who are available?"

 92

"But I *am* qualified!" I yelled out. Eva Longoria was back on screen, her tanned cleavage peeking out through a snug white T-shirt. She was mouthing off at someone, but I couldn't really focus, because my eyes were tearing up. My dad hit the MUTE button on the remote control.

"Indie, you might think that you are qualified in that you seem to know a great deal about fashion," he said. "But there are other things at work here, other things that people will never discuss with you."

I wiped my eyes and turned toward him.

"Dad, what are you talking about?" I asked, a note of irritation in my voice.

He took a deep breath.

"People like your lady, this Aaralyn, don't really associate with people like us. They might be friendly and civil and polite. They might come to us for dental checkups and chest exams or to have their taxes done. But they don't see us as their kind of people."

"You're babbling, Dad," I said. Actually, I knew what he was trying to tell me, but didn't want to agree with him. I thought back to that very first day, when I had accosted Aaralyn Taylor in the parking lot of my school as she was being driven away. When she had made that comment about people from "my part of the world" being good at "domestic duties." It had been, on the face of it, an insulting thing to say. Completely and utterly politically incorrect. She was looking down on me. But I was so desperate to be close to her, to find any way at all to work with her, that I had chosen to ignore it. Now my father, who wasn't even there, was able to express something that I hadn't been willing to confront.

"Think about it, Indie," he said, using the tone he employed with patients when he was trying to talk them into some kind of surgical procedure. "What kind of high-profile success have we, as a community, had in this country in the arts or media? Ismail Merchant made beautiful movies, but it's not like he was ever as well-known as Steven Spielberg. And that girl, that wonderful actress from *Bend It Like Beckham*, that Parminder Nagra—how many Americans even know her name? But her English sidekick on the movie goes on to Oscar nominations and all that."

I was impressed. My father, for all his professed disinterest in these things, was actually keeping track. He had obviously given this some thought.

"Look at Aishwarya Rai, the most famous person in all of India, the most beautiful," my father continued. "She appears on *60 Minutes*, even hires a Hollywood agent. There is talk of her being a Bond girl. Ha! It didn't happen. It could never happen! We are known for certain things and for those things only. Fashion and movies and the arts—in the minds of the average American, these are not our skills. And your Aaralyn, she is no different."

My mother emerged from the other room to tell me that

Kim was on the phone. I was relieved. I just wanted to get away from my dad and this uncomfortable conversation.

"I think she wants you to go over and watch a video at her house," my mother announced. "It's late, but because tomorrow is a holiday, I don't mind if you go. I'll drive you, if you want."

"Hey," I said, picking up the phone. That always drove my mother nuts, forcing her to ask me why I couldn't say hello "like normal people."

"Interested in seeing *Brokeback Mountain*?" Kim asked. "My mom won the DVD in some supermarket raffle."

"Not really," I said. "Gay cowboys, right?"

"Yeah, but I'd be totally into checking out some guy-on-guy action when the guys are as hot as those two," she said, giggling.

It wasn't my preferred choice of things to do, but I agreed.

I just needed to get out of the house.

As my mother drove me to Kim's, I replayed my dad's conversation in my mind. I didn't want to admit it, but he was right. The last time I had gone to India, one of my cousins had asked me if there was racism in America. My cousin, a wide-eyed thirteen-year-old girl, had read of such things.

"Especially after 9-11," she said. "That's what my teacher said."

I had grown up in America and saw myself as an American girl. Yes, I had that tongue-twisting name, got straight A's at school, and had the educated upper-middle-class parents, and therefore fit into every stereotype that most people might have of us. But I was American, really. I listened to Beyoncé and shopped at Wet Seal and hung out at the mall and spoke with no trace of an Indian accent.

But my father's words to me had reminded me of a thought I had the first time I saw Aaralyn Taylor's column at the front of her magazine. I imagined, in my prepubescent naïveté, having a similar column one day in a similar magazine. A photo of me would appear underneath, my skin dark and my hair black, and I would sign off, "Indie Konkipuddi, editor in chief."

Even then, somewhere in my psyche, it felt unreal.

Someone named Indie Konkipuddi stood virtually no chance of ever becoming editor of a high-flying magazine. We might be hardworking and competent and law-abiding, we might win book awards and direct good movies and run investment banks and even become Nobel laureates.

But we weren't the national news anchors, the chart-topping singing stars, the lead in a major Hollywood blockbuster. We worked quietly and did our jobs and then went home to our families. We spent American holidays with other Indians, eating *tandoori* chicken instead of roast turkey and not even considering throwing around a football afterward. We were Americans, but we didn't barbecue our meat on outdoor grills or sing carols or camp overnight outside Wal-Mart the day after Thanksgiving or *ever* drink milk with our meals.

In our house, we woke up every morning to *bhajans*—devotional Hindi songs. And my dad, no matter how late it was or how tired he felt, would end his day listening to something from his own boyhood in India, a lyrical and melancholy *raga* or an enduring classic from an old Bollywood film. These were the songs my parents grew up with and even though the bulk of my days were filled with MTV hits, those same days were bookended by songs that were nostalgic and soulful, linking my youth to that of my parents.

We were Americans but in name only. And although I had insisted on calling myself Indie, I still didn't have the right name for the job.

eleven

If I had been listening to my iPod, as I often was while walking to class, I wouldn't even have heard Brooke's softly spoken "hi."

I was strolling past her, making my way to second period, when she actually broke free from the clutch of girls she always hung out with and casually tossed that tiny word in my direction. Maybe she was going to comment on my outfit. I thought I looked especially awesome today. It was April—my favorite month because it was my birthday month—and I was wearing a top from Abercrombie & Fitch that still had its price tag on it that I had found at the local Goodwill. It shocked me what people tossed out. It was a charcoal-gray hoodie with a waist-tie and a slouchy pocket on the front. I wore it with leggings that had a lace trim that Kim had given me the previous Christmas. I had been horrified at the prospect of wearing leggings—after all, Hilary Duff I was not. But the length of the top covered my chunky thighs, and the fact that both pieces were the same color made me look leaner than I actually was. Around my neck I had strapped on a choker that I had made from one of my father's old belts, and on which I had sewn on tiny golden bells that often adorn Indian clothes. Kim had loved it so much she had offered to buy it from me. I told her I would get around to making her one.

But I was wondering why Brooke was saying "hi" to me today. The last time Brooke had talked to me was maybe a month and a half ago, on Valentine's Day. She had glided into school, carrying a single red rose adorned with a pink ribbon, which she said somebody had left on her doorstep that morning. She insisted she hadn't been able to find a bud vase at home and felt compelled to bring it to school. Then she stood in a corner with her gaggle of girls, showing them all the cards she had received that day—one, two, three . . . there were five. One contained two tickets to a movie, another a dried flower, another a slim silver chain. It had never occurred to me that teenage boys could be this romantic, but Brooke obviously brought out their better nature. She was beaming, enthralled. I had muttered "show-off" under my breath, gently patting my bag that contained the handmade card from my brother, which I knew he had only given to me because it was part of a class project.

"Lovely, aren't they?" she had said, glancing over in

my direction, fanning out the pink and red envelopes in front of her. I knew that she wasn't really talking to me, but just wanted to canvas as many witnesses as possible to the expressions of love before her.

So technically, Brooke had never really spoken to me. Maybe last week had changed that.

Truthfully, that weekend—the one where I had babysat Kyle at his mother's office—had changed everything. After I had come home from Kim's house, I just felt depressed. I had stared in the mirror for a while, looking at the face of the girl I thought I always knew, the girl who was mostly confident and had some sense of her place in the world.

But that evening, I could only see myself through Aaralyn's eyes. I didn't fit the mold, didn't have the kind of physical qualifications that would ever endear me to a woman like her. It didn't matter, I suddenly realized, that I had something of a unique sense of style. I didn't come from the right kind of family, didn't have those pretty light-skinned looks and willowy bodies of the girls that are employed by these magazines. I didn't have the connections or clout. I wasn't Brooke and never would be.

"Indie, right?" Brooke asked, a smile crossing her face.

Her friends, all equally gorgeous and blonde, stepped back, as if allowing their queen to assert herself.

"Aunt Aaralyn—although she hates it when I call her

that, tells me it makes her feel old—well, she said you were a real help to her."

"Oh really? That's good to know," I replied, hugging my textbooks close to my chest. "It was kinda fun. The kid's cute."

"Yes, little cousin Kyle. *Such* a darling. You know, Aunt Aaralyn keeps asking me to babysit, but I can never find the time," she said, now sighing as if the future of the world rested on her slender shoulders. "But now that you've done it and seem to be having fun at it, maybe I should reconsider."

I must have looked startled, because Brooke suddenly broke out into a fit of giggles.

"Oh please, don't worry," she said, a jeering tone in her voice. "I'm not going to take your precious babysitting job away from you. That would be just so *selfish*! What—and give you nothing else to look forward to on your weekends?"

Her friends all joined her now, giggling, and then together they all turned around and walked away. My face felt hot and I broke out into a little sweat all over my body. But I held my head up high, remembering Hinduism's karmic law that dictated that any act of cruelty in this life would result in some misfortune in the next. Not that I wanted to wish anyone ill, but Brooke Carlyle was known for being mean. So in her next incarnation, she'd probably come back as a rodent.

. . .

The little ring on my cell phone indicated a message, so when class was over, I checked my voice mail.

"Indie, beti, it's Mummy," my mother had recorded, feeling the need to identify herself. *"You. Call. Me. Please."* Every time my mother spoke into my voice mail, she sounded like she was speaking to someone who was deaf and couldn't utter a word of English. Something about it made her very uncomfortable. She was perhaps the least tech-savvy person I knew. In fact, it had only been recently that my mother had gotten herself an e-mail address and only at my insistence. Before that, she would stand behind me and dictate e-mails to her relatives overseas as I typed them in, using one of my handles. It was only when I told her she could download pictures of her newborn nephew in Kerala, or find reviews of the latest Hindi film online, that she finally agreed. Now, she spent a couple of hours a day on the computer; I had her hooked.

As soon as I got a chance, I called her back. I could imagine her, lounging in her favorite blue chair in the den, a cup of ginger tea by her side and a copy of *The Kite Runner* in her hands. I envied her ability to stick with all those hundreds of pages of any book, living with the characters for days or sometimes weeks on hand. She would often tell me that instead of wasting my time on the trivia inside *Celebrity Style*, it would benefit my mind more to read some of the literary world's great works. I knew she had a point: There really wasn't any contest between Charles Dickens and a two-page spread on whether Paris Hilton or Lindsay Lohan was hotter in the past year.

"What's up, Ma?" I asked her.

"Somebody just called for you. Junoon something. He left his number."

I laughed. I knew my mother was trying to tell me that it was Juno. It was funny that she had confused his name with the Hindi word for "obsession."

"Did he say what he wanted?"

"That he and his wife needed your help tonight with that baby. I don't know, Indie. You must be having homework and all, and your whole weekend was gone working for these people. You can't keep running there every time they call."

"Don't worry about it, Ma," I said. "Let me just give him a quick call back."

It was not inevitable, I knew, that Juno was calling me to ask me to babysit again, but I couldn't rationally think of what else it could be.

But something else had changed too; since my father's sobering talk from last weekend, I had been walking around with a sinking feeling in my stomach. I was beginning to realize that this thing I was doing with Aaralyn was a dead end for me. I was not much more than a passing convenience for her, and I could tell by the way she spoke to me that she didn't have that much regard for me.

And yet, a copy of my application for the internship at her magazine sat in a translucent folder adorned with glittery stickers on my bedside. Every night, I turned to look at it, read every word of the essay I had penned as to why I was the right person for the job, and every night I wondered if I could have said something else, something better, something different—something that would have caught the attention of the person it was sent to, who would then have sent it to Aaralyn with a strong recommendation that she hire me. Every night, I wondered if Aaralyn had ever even bothered to glance at it, and every night I considered tearing it up and tossing out the pieces.

But I had the good manners to call Juno back anyway.

There was a charity event that Aaralyn had decided to attend at the last minute, her husband was going to tag along, and their usual daytime nanny wasn't able to extend her hours to stay home with Kyle.

Juno's voice was pleading. "I know it's a school night, and it's a long way to come. And I really wouldn't ask if there was somebody else I could call. But there isn't. Aaralyn is dead set on going to this thing, and insists I go with her, although why she couldn't have figured this out last week is anybody's guess."

He sounded exasperated for a minute.

I *did* have a load of homework and had to start cramming massively for finals, although I told myself that I could always hit the books once Kyle was asleep.

"I'll have to ask my mom or dad if they can drive me," I said. "It's kind of a long way."

"I know," Juno said. "But if it helps, we can up your rate for today, seeing as it's a weeknight and all. Maybe ten an hour? Will that make it worth your while? And we'll throw in the gift bag from the event."

With an offer like that, there was no way I could say no.

My father, on the other hand, was not exactly part of the Coalition of the Willing. He was exhausted after a long day and the last thing he wanted to do was get back on the freeway.

"Indie, you are being taken advantage of and you are wasting your time and mine," he said when he got home, still standing in the doorway as I accosted him. "We have had this conversation already. You are squandering your talents. This is not a position you should be undertaking, and I will certainly not facilitate your ill-conceived ideas."

"But, Dad, please . . ." I started to beg. "They need me." I could feel myself tearing up again.

My mother appeared from the kitchen, holding a dishrag, a sprinkling of flour in her hair.

 105

"Rajiv, I can take her," she said. "This is important to her. Let her go."

"Nanda, when will you start putting your foot down?" my father asked. "She is still technically a child. We have the right, authority, and obligation to inform her when she is making a mistake."

"I agree with you, Rajiv. But this is something so important to her. Look at her face."

They both turned to look at me. Almost instinctively, and completely without guile, I had on my "poor me" look, the one I had as a child when I didn't get the Christmas present I was hoping for, the one that always surfaced when my father couldn't take me to Disneyland at the last minute because his pager went off and he had to rush off to the hospital.

"Remember, Rajiv, it is hard in this country to have children." My mother turned to look at me. "You know, Indie, if we were still in India when you were born, I would have given birth to you in my mother's house. You would have had grandparents, uncle, aunties, ayahs, and cooks. So many people to love you and care for you. But instead, I had you in an American hospital. And I remember how hard it was for me, your father busy all day, me trying to manage the housework and the cooking and a new baby. So I understand the needs of your Aaralyn."

I loved my mother.

She turned back to my father.

"You relax, Rajiv, I'll take her," my mother said, going back into the kitchen to put down the cloth. "You just remember, please, to take dinner out of the oven in forty minutes and then help Dinesh with his homework."

"Nanda, I don't want you driving by yourself at night," he said, perhaps forgetting that it was only five thirty.

"Okay, Indie," he said, resignation in his voice. "Get in the car."

When my dad pulled up to the house, Aaralyn's limo was already outside. I had to walk past it to get to her driveway. I recognized the driver from the day at the school, the day I had accosted her. If I hadn't done that, I wouldn't be here. The driver was outside the car, leaning up against it, reading the paper under a still-bright sky.

"Hello," I said, smiling. As I'd learned, it always paid to be nice to the help.

"Good evening," he said.

"I'm Indie," I replied. "I babysit Kyle."

"Aldo," he replied. "And yes, I remember you." His face took on a somewhat sardonic look. He probably thought I was a bit of a loser, running after a car like that.

Aaralyn was standing at the top of the stairs, wearing a silk slip, holding up two dresses in front of her husband who was halfway down the stairs.

"What do you think? Basic black or this orange? With my hair, the orange might be a bit much. I don't know why my stylist even bothered sending it over. Hi, Indie," she said as an afterthought. "Thanks for coming."

Kyle was nowhere to be seen, so I stood at the bottom of the steps, watching the exchange. I couldn't take my eyes off the dresses; the black was a Roland Mouret, curvy and clingy, one I'd just seen in a photograph somewhere on Scarlett Johansson. The second was Vera Wang, in sumptuous satin, a fuller skirt, and a sparkling flower at the waist.

"The orange," I said.

Juno turned to look at me, and Aaralyn was expressionless.

"It'll look amazing with your hair. Like Marcia Cross at the Golden Globes, remember? You'd be surprised. Just remove the flower thing. It'll break up the length, won't highlight your lean shape. And definitely metallic gold shoes—the Louboutins I glimpsed in there the other day."

I didn't know what had come over me. It wasn't as if I had consciously decided to speak. But the words just came out of my mouth, an outgrowth of the celebrity images I always carried around in my head.

"Juno, what do you think?" she asked. She completely ignored me, and I was suddenly embarrassed. What made me think Aaralyn Taylor would listen to me? Juno, noticing this exchange, looked up at his wife.

"The orange I think," he said, smiling.

Aaralyn studied the dress closely. "You might be right," she said to Juno. "Let me go and try it on."

When she emerged fifteen minutes later, accompanied by Juno in a smart black tuxedo, she was ravishing. She had left her hair down, her shiny tresses tumbling to her shoulders. Her makeup was simple yet striking.

"Don't look too impressed," she said. "My team left right before you got here. You didn't think that I could manage this all on my own, did you?"

She was wearing the beaded flower around her wrist, like a corsage. I thought it looked endearing, and would probably land her some space in any number of competing publications. But as she approached me, she took the flower off, and handed it to me.

"Here, for you," she said, thrusting it into my hand. The beads felt smooth against my palm, the soft silk scrunching against my skin. I had never even *seen* anything from Vera Wang except in the pages of a magazine, and here was I, not just *touching* it, but actually *owning* it.

"That might have some value on eBay," she said with a toss of her shiny hair. "Just in case you decide to sell it."

"Not in a million years," I replied, holding the flower to my chest as if it were a long-lost family heirloom.

Kyle had been upstairs with his parents the whole time, keeping himself amused as they got dressed. His father had carried him downstairs and now placed him gently in my arms. He didn't flinch, coming to me happily. "Dindy," he said, scratching my leather choker with his chubby fingers. I smiled. The boy was beginning to grow on me.

"Well, we're off," Juno said, glancing at his watch. "We should be home no later than eleven, if you want to call your dad. Oh, and by the way, if you hear any noise coming from my clinic out back, don't worry. It's my assistant, Cayman. He'll probably come in to get a sandwich."

"Cayman? As in the islands?" I asked, smiling.

"The very same," Juno replied. "His parents are terminally trendy. They still go to rock concerts. They went to Burning Man in the desert last year—you know, that totally radical, cultish, artsy extravaganza."

I had seen a bit about Burning Man on the news and knew what Juno was talking about. Assuming that his parents and mine were of the same generation, I couldn't even imagine my folks at something like that. The most radical thing they had done in recent memory was attend a barn dance that was a fund-raiser for Dinesh's school, and even then, had spent most of the evening sitting on the sidelines, drinking free Gatorade.

"Call if there's a problem," Aaralyn said, making sure her cell phone was tucked inside her bejeweled clutch. "But," she continued, tossing me a stern look, "try not to."

I carried Kyle back into the kitchen, stuck him in his high chair, and started getting his dinner ready. There was some boiled squash in a pot on the stove, a couple of chunks of avocado covered in plastic wrap on the counter, and mushy brown rice in another dish. I put fresh water in his sippy cup, pulled up a chair and started singing to him as I fed him.

"I've never heard Maroon 5 that way," said a voice behind me.

Startled, I turned around and figured that this must be Cayman. He looked like his name. There was something breezy and relaxed about him. A mop of tousled golden-brown hair came down to just below his ears, matching the color of his eyes. He had a wide smile, broken only by a tiny gap between his two front teeth. Around his neck was a leather string, in the middle of which was suspended a cowrie shell. He was wearing a beige linen shirt over khakis, a pair of Timberlands on his feet.

It looked to me as if he had inherited the "terminally trendy" gene.

"Hey, I'm Cayman," he said. "Juno's part-time assistant."

"Indie," I replied, extending my hand and half standing up. "Kyle's sometime babysitter."

"I like the song," he said, referring to what I'd just been warbling, terribly out of tune.

"*She will be loved.* Great thing to sing to a kid, even if he doesn't understand a word of it. But I like that you changed the 'she' to 'you.' Sweet."

He grinned again.

"I was going to order in some Chinese food. Hungry?"

twelve

Cayman Roos was, by far, the coolest kid I had ever met.

As we munched on Szechuan chicken, fried rice, and egg rolls, and drank from huge tankards of Diet Coke filled with ice, he told me all about the fascinating things he was doing during his year off, before starting college. As Kyle slept upstairs, Cayman filled me in on the scuba diving instructing he had done off the Cayman Islands, which made me laugh when he talked about it. He had worked for a company that gave hot-air balloon rides over Temecula wine country. He had spent a month teaching surfing in Molokai in Hawaii.

I was amazed by it all: The farthest I had ever gotten was to Calcutta, which my parents and I would visit every two years, my father cashing in all his frequent flyer miles for four tickets. I always longed to do something else—even travel around India a little bit. But between two sets of grandparents and more aunts and uncles than I could count, our summers always came to an end, and we'd be ready to return to the hills of Agoura, loaded down with so much luggage that we'd often be scrambling at the airport, removing big jars of pickles and wooden statues from our suitcases and sending them back to my grandparents' place with the driver. Even so, we'd end up using every pound of luggage allowance we had, and would carry on so many bags that my father used to say that we looked like refugees.

Cayman was telling me that his adventures had to stop after a while. "My parents are pretty open, but they thought I was wasting a lot of time. Which I was, of course." He smiled.

They suggested he do something more constructive, something to help prepare him for medical school. So he scrolled through Craigslist and came across an ad placed by Juno for a part-time personal assistant.

"There was something about the way he phrased the ad, something that was honest and to the point, so I thought I'd check it out," Cayman recalled. "When I met him, I figured it would be a great way to spend the rest of my year. My parents have always been interested in alternative healing—Dad hasn't taken so much as an aspirin in five years. So I come in for several hours a few times a week, plan Juno's schedule, take appointments, deal with his billings and the insurance companies, that kind of thing. It's great. I'm earning my own money so I don't feel so bad still living in the bedroom next to my parents. And Juno is a really nice guy, even though his wife is a bit crazy."

I realized that this was the longest I had ever spoken to any boy before. At fifteen going on sixteen, I had never had a date. My father, a year earlier, had given me a really awkward "there will come a time" talk, about boys and girls and love and romance, never quite making any points, just meandering aimlessly through examples and anecdotes I didn't understand.

"I know we are in America, where everyone dates, even as young as you," my dad had said. "I want you to know that I am not against such a concept. But I do wish that you wouldn't do it."

My father didn't have much to worry about in that regard. While there had been a couple of boys in school that I had liked and one that I had even had a huge crush on last year, none of them had liked me back. This was a vastly different scenario from the other girls in the school, the Brookes and their ilk, who talked about the boys they had made out with, giggling as they recounted all the details of a frenzied night of passion in the back of a car. I could only imagine what that felt like. To me, "first base" was actually a sporting term. It didn't surprise me then that these girls tended to keep these conversations to themselves, lowering their voices in the changing room as I walked by, knowing that there was no way that I could even understand.

They were probably right. Where they had all done God knows what with a boy, I couldn't even get someone to slow dance with me. At a dance a month earlier, where the theme was eighties disco, I sat on top of the stage, twirling the pendant that hung from a red silk rope around my neck, hoping and praying someone would ask me to dance while, fittingly, ABBA's "Dancing Queen" played out of the DJ booth. But the only person who I hung out with was Kim. So we hung around and dissected everyone's wardrobe and I pretended not to care that not a single boy had come to talk to me, while I secretly wished that I could dance and jive and have the time of my life.

So if there ever had been an ideal boy for me, Cayman would be it. He was funny and smart and not boisterous like so many other guys his age. He didn't sit there and chew gum and unconsciously twirl a pen in his hand as he made a phony attempt to have a conversation with me. He had a direct gaze, asked me great questions about my life, and really seemed to listen. He was seventeen and planning to go to medical school. If only he was Indian, my father would love him.

Just as we were polishing off the last of the egg rolls, Aaralyn and Juno walked through the door.

"Hey, Cayman, you're still here!" Juno announced. "I see you found some company," he said, smiling in my direction.

Aaralyn ignored both of them, asking me immediately what time Kyle had fallen asleep, if he had finished is dinner, if he had had a bowel movement.

"Okay, I think that's my sign to leave," said Cayman, gathering the boxes of Chinese takeout and carting them to the trash can in the kitchen.

We left at the same time, Cayman getting into his white Mazda parked outside.

"Great meeting you," Cayman said, as I walked toward my father.

"Maybe I'll see you around?" he said.

"That'd be amazing," I replied.

thirteen

My sixteenth birthday cake was in the shape of a clothes hanger. I could see what my mother had tried to do, but wished she could have been a little more inventive, maybe seeking out a confectioner who could render a spun-sugar version of a Balenciaga bag or an Elie Saab gown, or a chocolate cake in the shape of a pair of Marc Jacobs ballerina flats.

But a clothes hanger it was, painted in bright red food coloring atop a vanilla surface, my name on a tag where the price might be, a *1* and *6* candle put together.

My birthday was on April 12, a date that I was thrilled to share with the ever-stylish Claire Danes, although my father was far more excited that some ancient Bollywood actor and director called Kidar Nath Sharma was born on the same day as me.

But this birthday was special. For two weeks, the fact that I was turning sixteen was about the only thing anyone in my family talked about. If I ever felt the need to sulk, my mother would tersely remind me that I "was about to turn sixteen, and it was time to start acting like a grown-up." In my father's mind, it was when I would have to start getting serious about my plans for college, indeed for the rest of my life. In my family, the age marked a rite of passage in a way. It was the age, my mother loved telling me, that her own parents started to talk to her about how she would marry someday and have a family of her own. The day she turned sixteen, she was allowed to wear lipstick, to go out to the coffee shop down the street with her friends without a parent chaperoning them. It was when she was allowed to watch more adult-themed movies, when she had permission to shut the door to her bedroom when she was in it, knowing that her parents had to knock if they wanted to come in.

Being in America and going to a private high school filled with the mostly spoiled children of pretty well-off families, I was a bit beyond all that. I had been wearing lipstick—okay, lip gloss—since I was twelve, and Kim and I often hung out at the local food court at the mall on our own. Here in America, we grow up early.

But still, I was excited about going out to dinner with my family. While we dined together at home almost every night, going out to a restaurant was still a special occasion. That was a throwback to life in the old country.

My parents had grown up with enough money, but not a lot, and eating out was a luxury rarely indulged. They had brought that with them when they moved to America, my mother loving to tell us that whatever it was we wanted, she could make at home for next to nothing.

Most of my friends who had already turned sixteen saw it as another milestone; it meant that they could drive. Oddly, that had never been on my list of priorities. I had thought that might change given my new "situation" with Aaralyn, that I would no longer have to rely on either one of my parents to drive me back and forth.

But something about getting behind the wheel of a car had always scared me a little. Every time I had seen someone make a dicey left turn, or merge into a busy freeway, I had felt terrified. And it didn't help that my parents had not necessarily encouraged me toward driving either. My mother had waited two full years to get her license after coming to America. She had never understood why it was so important in this country for a child to drive at sixteen or to move out at eighteen.

"You will do what you need to do when you are ready," she had said. I had felt comforted by that.

We had a tradition in my family which I had always loved, and that was that on a person's birthday, no voices should be raised at them, no tone used other than one of love and reverence. My brother and I could rob a bank or set the school on fire, and my parents would gaze at us lovingly and smilingly. I should probably take more advantage of it.

So my mother had driven me to the mall the day earlier and had allowed me to spend up to fifty dollars on a new outfit. To me, that was a relative fortune. A lot of the girls in school were routinely given hundreds of dollars by their parents to buy whatever they wanted. But I was on a strict budget, my father wanting to cultivate in me an innate value for money.

"But *Dad*, a girl in my class was wearing these *really hot* Candie's wedge-heeled shoes," I told him once.

"You know, your grandfather, my father, had *no* shoes at all!" he would reply. "Nothing! Barefoot he walked to school!"

The inevitability of the response always made me giggle.

But now, fifty dollars for a birthday ensemble? He was only too happy to oblige.

While my mother had waited outside the changing room, I tried on several dresses and finally settled on a white halter-neck with a pretty black lace print all over the front. It was under twenty dollars, leaving me money for a pair of shoes and new bag. I went with flat gladiator sandals and a framed clutch that had a lovely vintage feel to it, my mother reminding me that her own mother used to carry similar clutches back in the day in Calcutta, and they could be found for pennies at the local market. I realized then that I would most likely be forever haunted by examples of my simple, earthy, unassuming grandparents.

After I had finished getting dressed for dinner, both my parents had beamed in my general direction. I even thought that my mother would start crying.

"You look all grown up," she said as if she hadn't seen me since I was in preschool. "Sixteen! Where have the years gone?"

My mother had carted along the cake in a huge white box, wanting to surprise me with it, but knowing it was impossible because I was riding along in the car with them.

"It's nothing!" she laughed, when I asked her what it was, knowing full well. "Mind your own business, birthday girl!"

I thought about all this with gratitude as we got ready to go to Paulie's Kitchen, a restaurant near our house, a place that we always went to for family celebrations—birthdays, anniversaries, reunions with relatives visiting from India. It was our special event place.

It was at times like these that I was at my happiest: when the restaurant staff would emerge from the kitchen, carrying the cake with its lit candles, singing "Happy Birthday" in off-key voices, my parents joining in and sounding equally off. Everyone's eyes glowed beneath the red-covered lamp above our table. For that one moment, we were all together, wishing for the very best, everything else pushed aside. They were times that spoke of family, about more than clothes and fashion and who was wearing what. They were, I supposed, the only times in my life when I didn't even mind if anyone called me Indira.

fourteen

Gina Troy wasn't on the cover of the next *Celebrity Style*. Instead, there was a story about Reese Witherspoon moving on with her life post-Ryan, something I had read and reread everywhere. Inside, in the pages where I gathered there would have been a blow-by-blow on Gina Troy's wedding attire, on the Badgley Mischka gown and the Stuart Weitzman shoes that I had seen photographed on GossipAddict.com, there was instead a feature on the resurgence of the clog, which I had to admit was only mildly interesting.

Who cared about clogs?

It was one of the least interesting issues of the magazine I had ever read. Instead of the latest and hottest news, everything seemed old and rerun.

I couldn't help but wonder what was going on with Aaralyn. I hadn't heard from her or Juno for a couple of weeks. I had babysat Kyle for three weekends in a row, and when I had mentioned that my birthday was coming up, Aaralyn had handed over a bag containing beauty products from Pout and Fresh and Bliss, which I knew that she probably didn't buy and were most likely sent to her by the companies, but I loved them anyway. She probably kept a stash at home, for occasions just like these.

But then two weeks had passed, and nothing. I had considered calling her, to make sure everything was okay with them and Kyle. But part of me felt that was intrusive. I was, after all, the hired help. I wasn't a friend, right?

As I lounged around at home on a Saturday morning, every time my phone rang on a weekend, part of me hoped it would be Aaralyn or Juno, asking me to come by and watch Kyle. I thought I had been doing well, was slowly getting into their good graces. I had also tried to forget what my father had said to me weeks earlier. That whole conversation seemed to have faded into the background. Or perhaps my father simply assumed that Aaralyn and her family had moved on and no longer required my services. For my part, I didn't know what to think. But the silence was disconcerting, especially since there were barely six weeks left before the intern would be announced and school was out. I still didn't know where things stood for the summer.

I had to confess there was something else too. Cayman. In the past few weeks, I had thought many times about that night he and I shared Chinese food, about the easy way we talked and laughed. In that one evening, I had developed a huge crush on him, and I hadn't really crushed on anybody since Ace Young on *American Idol*. At least Cayman was a person I could see again—if only the Taylors would call.

My mild depression was compounded by the fact that Kim had somehow gone and found herself a boyfriend. Brett was in school with us, and I had known that Kim had really liked him, but I always saw Kim to be like me: crushing on boys that she could never have. I had figured that she, like me, would probably never kiss anyone until she was in college.

Brett was decent enough, so I didn't discourage Kim's infatuation with him. He didn't take drugs or seem to be the kind of guy who would ever show up at school with an Uzi. In the past, he had just never seemed to notice her, uttering no more than a throwaway "hey" every now and again. I figured she'd get over him before long.

But everything had changed last week, and I was there at the precise moment it happened.

It was lunch period, and we were hanging out in one of the hallways comparing shoes, and Kim's brand-new magenta RAZR cell phone rang, loudly broadcasting the song she had just downloaded from Lil Scrappy. Brett happened to be walking past and his cell rang at the exact same moment with the exact same song.

"Dude, you got 'Money in the Bank' too," he said,

saying more to her then than ever before. "The song is kick-ass."

Kim beamed at him, stuttered for a second, and then gathered herself quickly enough to initiate a conversation about Scrappy's new album. I stood there, smiling at both, unable to contribute to the conversation.

They hit the mall the next evening and had hung out together ever since, united by something as meaningless as a temporary ring tone. I didn't want to be jealous, but I was; not because Brett was anything special, but because Kim had finally joined the ranks of the girls who dated, and I was still left behind, sitting around at home on a Saturday with nothing more than a plan to accompany my parents to lunch at the home of one of their friends.

My cell rung at that moment, and my caller ID told me it was Kim.

"Hey," I said. "I was just thinking about you."

"'Sup?" she replied. It always made me laugh when Kim tried be more cool than she was. She was also recently experimenting with ultra-hip clothing pieces that even I didn't have the courage to try out. With her straight hair and generally bland features, ripped denim jackets covered in chains and skinny camouflage-print leggings looked a little silly.

"Not much," I replied. "You?"

"Just chillin'," she said. I thought she had been watching too much BET.

"I thought you might be Aaralyn. Haven't babysat in two weeks. Weird," I said.

"Oh hey, I heard something about her," she replied.

I sat up. Being the gossip fiend that I was, those were my favorite words in the whole world. That, and "warehouse sale."

"About Aaralyn? How? What?" I asked anxiously.

"I was with Brett at Stone Cold Creamery last night," Kim said, a tinge of pride in her voice. "His friend Tyler was there too. You remember Tyler, right?"

"Vaguely," I replied, recalling another moderately good-looking, moderately boneheaded boy in the Brett vein.

"Well, guess who else was there? Brooke Carlyle. The line was humongous—you know what it's like on a Friday night. So I stayed outside to grab a table. Later, Tyler said that Brooke told him she was about getting ready to intern at *Celebrity Style* over the summer."

My heart stopped.

"But, like, she was saying that things looked iffy at the magazine, that her aunt has been really stressed out," Kim continued. "That Aaralyn chick is crazier than usual. Brooke can't even pin her down for a few minutes. Aaralyn and that husband of hers, the one with the hippy-dippy name, they've been away a lot. They've been dropping off the kid with a relative, and going off to Palm Springs, Santa Barbara. Their marriage is dying, baby."

"Oh my God," I replied. "That would explain a lot.

Listen, I *have* to hear more about this. Wanna grab a bite somewhere? I'll see if someone can drive me."

My dad agreed to drop me off at the strip mall Starbucks that was midway between Kim's house and mine. He was on his way to Home Depot with Dinesh, to look for tiles for a kitchen remodel he was about to attempt on his own, after being inspired by something he'd seen on HGTV. He had made these efforts before, and they usually resulted in a pile of materials sitting in our garage, expensive tools still in their boxes, and not a lick of work done with any of it.

But my arrangement to meet Kim worked out perfectly, actually. Kim was going to go hang with Brett later, and said she would use me as her alibi, like she always did. Her parents thought she was too young to date, and they said they didn't want her to go out alone with any guy until she was at least in college, so I had been covering for her. So far, she hadn't gotten caught, but I did tell her it was only a matter of time. But the secrecy surrounding their relationship had seriously helped in this instance. Nobody knew that Brett was dating Kim, which is why Brooke stood in line as she waited for her cheesecake ice cream with graham cracker pie crust and talked about Aaralyn's problems.

She probably wouldn't have if she had known that Tyler's friend's girlfriend's best friend happened to be after the same job.

. . .

Brett showed up at Starbucks just as Kim and I were getting tucked into our Caramel Macchiatos, still steaming hot, the foaming milk on top sprinkled with cinnamon. We had elected to split a slice of lemon Bundt cake, which I knew was a very wicked thing to do, but I was bored and distracted and couldn't help myself. Still, I soothed my guilt around it by reminding myself that at least I was sharing it.

Kim stood on her toes to kiss her boyfriend. It was weird, seeing her lips touch his. My first instinct was to turn away as if I were crashing some intimate moment.

"I'm early," Brett announced. "So I'm gonna hang with you."

"Sure," I said, smiling politely.

"So Brett, Indie wanted to know what you heard last night," Kim said, launching straight into it.

"About what?" he asked.

"You know, that thing you told me, about what Brooke Carlyle said last night. About her aunt and that magazine."

"You tell her, babe," he said to Kim. He then reached into the sleek gray bag he had had slung across his body and pulled out a portable media player. I couldn't believe it; Kim's new boyfriend was going to sit there and watch TV. What a catch he turned out to be.

Kim turned back to me, visibly embarrassed.

"Okay, I'll just tell you what this guy—" she motioned to her boyfriend with her thumb—"told me yesterday." Brett, his eyes affixed to the screen, headphones on, was oblivious.

"Brooke was just going on about really expecting to work at that magazine this summer," she continued. "But her aunt is totally MIA, not calling her back. The magazine's going through a rough patch. Not good all around. Brett told me that Tyler was doing most of the listening or at least pretending to listen. He was faking it because he's really into that girl. She's pretty hot, I guess."

Brett, obviously at the end of whatever show he was watching, removed his headphones and turned his attention back to us.

"You done discussing that bogus stuff?" he asked.

We both nodded obediently.

"Good," he said, putting his gadget away. "Come on, Kim," he said. "Let's get outta here."

fifteen

As soon as my shiny new issue of *Celebrity Style* arrived, the first one for the month of May, I took it upstairs to read in the privacy of my bedroom. The cover story was a compilation of celebrity weddings, and included a small item on Gina Troy. I leaped ahead to the fashion section, which was my favorite part of the magazine. I usually loved it for the "Headliners" section, where it would give stars to fashion items—five for the piece that was the trendiest, the prettiest, the best value for money—and one star for some awful number that a fashion victim actress/model had thrown on for some event. It was a great page—informative, witty, and easy to read.

But the entire section was missing.

I went back to the index at the front, and looked for it, checking all the pages again carefully, but it wasn't there. I flicked through a few more pages, looking for the column called "Frisk," where a staff writer would corner a celebrity at an event or even out on the street, and ask them what they had on—from the make of their watch to their underwear. It was always revealing and insightful to learn that some A-list hottie had found a skirt for five dollars at a Salvation Army store, but had thrown it together with some stylist-provided designer dud. I loved it, because in my mind, that was what fashion was all about—letting the clothes speak for themselves.

But that wasn't there either.

Instead, there was a note at the back of the magazine saying: HEADLINERS AND FRISK ARE TAKING A BREAK, AND WILL BE BACK SHORTLY.

What was going on?

I then remembered my conversation with Kim from the other day.

I had been so enamored of the magazine—of the beautiful pictures and the gorgeous gowns—that I had forgotten to take into account that it was a business like any other, a business that needed new ideas and good people.

That whole week in school, I had been finding it very hard to concentrate on anything. Mr. Fogerty had already lost his patience with me twice during class, once when I had forgotten to bring my homework in, and another time when I was telling Kim about the latest disappointing issue of *Celebrity Style* in the middle of Mr. Fogerty's talk on identifying acidic oxides in the atmosphere. Any other time, I might have been vaguely interested. But I couldn't get Aaralyn out of my head. I had actually started to become strangely sympathetic toward her, wondering how she was coping with everything that was happening. And then of course, I thought rather selfishly, if I never saw Aaralyn again, I'd probably never see Cayman again either. I felt a little pinprick of disappointment.

"*Indira!*" he said, as I was in mid-sentence with Kim. "Is this something you'd like to share with the rest of the class?"

I shook my head meekly, all the while wanting to blurt out to Mr. Fogerty that everyone in this class would rather hear about the soap opera goings-on at the Taylor household rather than what happens when chromium trioxide reacts with water.

At nine that night, while I was helping my mom with the dishes, my cell rang.

"Hi, Indie, it's Aaralyn," she said. Her voice didn't sound as sharp as it had in the past, it was more subdued, more tempered.

"Hello, how are you?" I asked, trying to sound nonchalant, as if I had no idea that she was apparently on the verge of a nervous breakdown.

"Fine," she said curtly. "We've been away a lot. But I could use your help tomorrow afternoon. From two to seven. Can you make it?"

"I think so," I said, realizing after I hung up that I

should probably have asked my parents first to see who could drive me.

"Tomorrow is not possible," my father said sternly, when I checked with him. "How could you forget?"

I had a blank expression on my face. What had I forgotten?

"Tomorrow is Aditya's wedding," my father said, raising his voice. "We are all expected there."

Aditya was the son of very good friends of my parents. He was twenty-one and had met his fiancée at UC Berkeley. I think my father had been secretly hoping that Aditya would have remained single into his mid-twenties, so that he and I could eventually have gotten together. But because he was now old enough to drink while I was still a teenager, Aditya had never paid any attention to me. I could see what my father liked in him though; he was tall, good-looking, and well-spoken, and was on his way toward a degree in bioengineering. He had apparently expressed an interest in restaurants and culinary arts, but his father, who was like mine in so many ways, had said something along the lines of: "No son of mine will become a kitchen boy!" And so Aditya had changed his mind and had conceded to poaching eggs in his spare time instead of as a career. His fiancée, Sumitra, who was from an equally pedigreed family, had been majoring in earth and planetary science. They would no doubt have extremely well-qualified children. I thought they were far too young to be married but seeing as my parents were that age when they got hitched, I didn't really have much heft to my argument.

"Dad, I'm sorry, I completely forgot," I said, by way of explanation.

"Uh-oh, you're in *trrr-ooo—bbel*," Dinesh said, his voice tuning into an annoying singsong one that he reserved for moments such as these.

"How could you forget? We have been talking about nothing else all week," my mother said, dropping a chopstick onto the table. "Why, just the other night, I showed you two saris and asked you to help me choose one. Remember?"

I did, vaguely. But with the dramas at the Taylor residence playing out in my mind, and my mild but completely pointless infatuation with Cayman, I had been preoccupied lately.

"What time is the ceremony? And where is it again?" I asked my mother.

"Eleven. And lunch right after," she said. "At the temple in Malibu."

"I can do that," I replied, feeling slightly relieved. "Aaralyn said she wouldn't need me till two. So I can come to the ceremony, have a quick bite afterward, and then maybe one of you can drive me to Brentwood?" I asked, a begging tone creeping unbidden into my voice.

My parents looked at each other.

"Indira, we cannot just disappear," said my father. "It is rude. This is a big community celebration. Everyone will be there, including Rinky, Tinky, and Pinky. *Those* girls will be there start to finish, socializing nicely with everyone."

"Dad, they just have nothing better to do," I said, regretting the words as soon as they came out of my mouth.

"And you? You think you have something better to do by rushing off and cleaning some boy's bottom?" he asked, now getting irritated. "How will it look that you just eat and run? And what will we tell everyone when they ask where you have gone? And what makes you think that we will want to tear ourselves away and drive forty miles to take you somewhere you shouldn't even be?"

"So you're telling me no?" I asked, tears beginning to gather in my eyes.

"It is just too rushed, *beta*," my mother said, her tone softer than that of my father. "We will barely have any time there if we have to leave by one to take you somewhere. You just tell Aaralyn that this time, you cannot come."

I burst into tears on the spot. Dinesh came up from behind, the childish smirk gone from his face, and wrapped his skinny arm around my waist. When my father left the room, my mother approached me, and gently swept a tendril of my hair behind my ear.

"Indie, I have tried to be supportive of your choice to do this work. You know this, yes?' Her face was soft in the pale glow of an overhead lamp, and her fingers smelled vaguely of turmeric. "I can see your father's side, but I can also see yours. We have always made it possible for you to go and help that woman, even when she calls you at the very last moment. But tomorrow, Indie, it is just not possible. You have to remember your obligations to us as well."

I nodded silently, wiped away my tears, and went upstairs to call Aaralyn back.

"We have a family function to attend tomorrow," I said to her. "Even if I can leave early to get to you by two, my parents want to stay. Basically, I have nobody to drive me." I felt foolish, like a useless, dependent child.

Aaralyn sighed deeply.

"Well, I can't find anybody else at this late stage, so we're going to have to try and make this work, aren't we?" she asked, her voice irate. Why was she blaming me?

"I guess I could send a car for you. But can someone at least pick you up from here after?"

seventeen

It felt odd getting all dolled up in gold and silks in the middle of the morning, at a time when our neighbors were working in their gardens or going for a jog or reading their papers at the nearby Coffee Bean & Tea Leaf.

At home, we were emerging from our bedrooms in full regalia. My mother had opted for the cream Banarasi silk sari on my recommendation. It came with a thick gold border in a paisley pattern, and small fleur-de-lis-type patterns all over the rest of the fabric. My mother, of course, had no idea what either of those terms meant.

My father appeared in an embroidered beige silk *kurta* with a matching waistcoat and pants. His hair was slicked back, he had replaced his glasses with contact lenses, and all in all looked very handsome. Even Dinesh, who was wearing a micro version of my father's outfit, looked the opposite of his usual scruffy, skateboarding self.

I, of course, had sat in front of my closet for fifteen minutes earlier that morning, trying to figure out what to wear. I had to take into consideration not only the fact that the entire community was going to be there, but that it was going to be in a temple—which meant that as much as I wanted to, I couldn't really jazz up any of my outfits like I usually did. And although I rarely wore a sari, I had a few hanging in my closet, gifted to me by my relatives in India who hoped ardently that I would one day grow my hair long, dump the rubber wristbands and mohair shrugs, and become, as they liked to say: "a graceful Indian girl."

No time like the present, I thought to myself.

When I stepped out of my bedroom, my mother actually gasped. There was no up-and-down staring and a "what are you wearing?" look on her face. There was no exasperation from my father, who hated my oversize sweaters, thick belts, and the way I mangled a *dupatta*. Even Dinesh, who never really noticed me at all, said, "Hey, Indie, you look nice."

I had decided to wear a *lehenga*—yet another permutation of an Indian ensemble. It was a full-bodied ankle-length skirt teamed with a short, fitted blouse and a large piece of sheer fabric draped across it. The one I had chosen was in a *bandini* design—a very traditional Indian print that had recently become popular in the West; it was like tiny, multicolored polka dots, arranged over the crushed silk fabric, with gold beads sprinkled over them. I had put on a fairly ornate gold necklace and earring set, a *bindi* on my forehead, anklets at my feet. Even my shoes—raw silk embellished with beads—had been bought in Calcutta and were as conventional as they come. I usually paired them with clam-diggers and a draped tee, but now, adding the finishing touch to my thoroughly traditional gear, I had to confess that they actually looked very attractive.

"Now *this* is more like it," my father said, walking around me as if I were a piece of art that he was considering buying. "All these lovely clothes that your relatives have bought for you over the years—at long last they are coming to good use, not being taken apart in the usual nonsensical way."

"Thanks, Dad," I said.

I was in a very good mood. I was going to the wedding, thereby pleasing my family, and then would be picked up by Aaralyn's driver Aldo at one p.m. My father had agreed to fetch me from Brentwood at seven, giving him more than enough time to socialize at the wedding and lunch.

Everyone was happy.

Of all the "inkys," Rinky was the least obnoxious. Maybe it was because she was the oldest of the trio, but she had always seemed to have more common sense than the other two put together. And unlike her two younger sisters, she also displayed more of an interest in the world around her, occasionally stopping to glance at the *Daily News* or even turning her radio to 102.7, with all its pop music and gossip news. I had always thought there would be some hope for her.

We made our way into the main hall, which was slowly filling up. It was part of my nature to take in what the other women were wearing, and I was pleasantly surprised. Astounded, actually. Here before me were not just the typical saris and *salwar kameez* ensembles, but an array of terrifically fashionable Indian clothes. I had known that India was becoming a bonafide fashion capital, that there was even an Indian Fashion Week, just like they have in London, Milan, New York, and Paris. And there were plenty of girls here who obviously followed those trends as much as I followed Western ones. There were flowing palazzo pants with lace inserts paired with short embroidered tunics, and heavily embellished halter-neck blouses set off with a simple sari. One woman was wearing a satin *ghagra choli*—a cropped top, flared skirt, and matching shawl—that was in the most divine shade of chocolate, studded with turquoise stones and accented with raffia. Being surrounded by women in the latest styles fresh off a Delhi designer catwalk, my outfit suddenly felt dated and boring. I knew I should have mixed it up a bit, added a bit of my own attitude to it, instead of wearing it traditionally.

Obviously, classic Indian garb just wasn't cool anymore.

It was just before eleven, and there was no sign of the couple, although the priest was sitting cross-legged on the floor, preparing for the ritual: arranging pieces of red cloth, a brown-haired coconut, chunks of rock sugar, a tin of ghee.

"Come, let's all sit together," Rinky said, tugging at my hand.

We found empty spots on the cold marble floor, and virtually piled up on top of one another, all of us a flurry of silks and brocades and jangling jewelry. The inhabitants of the hall were in full conversation mode, jovially greeting one another and exchanging news about their health, the weather, a relative visiting from India, gas prices. They could have been anywhere, instead of in this hall that was slowly growing warmer and more crowded.

The thing hadn't even started yet, and I couldn't wait for it to end. I anxiously looked at my watch—it was eleven fifteen. I had left a change of clothes in the car and was hoping to have a few minutes sometime before Aldo showed up to get into them.

"What's the rush?" Rinky asked, obviously noticing the anxiety on my face. "Going somewhere? Meeting somebody?"

"Kind of," I replied. "I do have somewhere to get to in a couple of hours."

"How's your babysitting job?" she asked, not making much of an effort to hide the look of condescension on her face.

"It's not a job, really. And it's fine," I replied, trying to uphold my dignity. "The people there are very nice." I thought of Cayman for a minute and smiled to myself.

"I know your parents don't think very much of it, but it's good that you're doing what you want to do," Rinky said, her tone suddenly changing and becoming more serious. "It's a little unusual for us type of girls, but there's really nothing wrong with it."

"I know that," I said, appreciating her efforts. "What about you? How are your plans coming along to visit India this summer? That all sounded pretty cool, what you wanted to do there."

"It's happening," she said, flipping her hair with one hand. "We've made our bookings and everything is set up. Although of course, with India, you never know how anything is going to turn out." She paused for a second, as if recalling something related to what she was doing, but not quite.

"Oh, but it should be interesting at Mother Teresa's mission in Calcutta while we're there. Trixie Van Alden is stopping by."

I drew in a sharp intake of breath. Trixie Van Alden was the name on everyone's lips these days. An Oscar-winning A-list star, she had been in all the headlines lately because she had run off with a much-married megastar. They were now engaged and were planning a wedding later in the year, the photographs of which were estimated to cost in the millions of dollars, if not more, for any publication who could afford them. But even more significantly than the mystery date and venue of the wedding was what Trixie Van Alden was going to wear; every fashion designer from Giorgio Armani to Roberto Cavalli was flinging frocks at her, desperate for her to choose one of them. The last I had read in *Celebrity Style* a few weeks ago, she was leaning toward Christian Lacroix Couture. It was an unconventional choice. But Trixie Van Alden was an unconventional woman.

"Why is she going to a mission in Calcutta?" I asked. The room had begun to quiet down because the couple, at last, had entered. Rinky and her sisters were fixated on them, gazing at Sumitra's heavily embroidered red-and-gold sari, and at Aditya's thick silk burgundy *shervani*—the traditional bridegroom costume. They were arranging themselves on the floor atop rugs, preparing for the ritual of endless Sanskrit words that I would never be able to comprehend.

"Rinky, why is Trixie Van Alden going to Calcutta?" I asked again. But the three sisters all looked at me simultaneously, each one raising a finger to their lips, and let out a long "Ssshhhh."

It felt interminable. When, finally, the bride and groom stood up to walk around the fire, I figured that possibly, at long last, the ceremony was drawing to an end. Finally, there would be lunch—and more important, a chance to finish my conversation with Rinky.

The priest finally stood up, signifying that the ceremonial part of the day was over and it was now time to congratulate the couple and their respective families. Rinky, who by now had attached herself to her own parents, began moving toward Aditya and Sumitra, joining the crowd that was working its way toward them.

But my curiosity had obviously gotten the better of me. I grabbed on to Rinky's hand, my palm clasping the dozen glass bangles wrapped around her slender wrist.

"Come on, Rinky, you didn't tell me the whole story. What is Trixie Van Alden doing in India?"

Rinky blinked.

"Oh, *now* you're interested in talking to me, are you?" There was a sarcastic note to her voice, but she kept a smile on her face, softening her tone.

"Look, I'm just interested, all right? Fine, don't tell me if you don't want to. See if I care." I knew I was sounding petulant, but I didn't want to give Rinky the satisfaction of seeing how much I wanted to hear what she had to say. It was like we were still in preschool.

"Well, you know Madhu Sharma, the lady at the India Association here who helps organize for Americans to visit one of the missions in Calcutta?" she whispered.

I nodded vaguely. Madhu Sharma was one of those

bossy Indian ladies who always wore her hair in a bun and talked in an unnecessarily loud voice. She looked down on girls in the community who expressed any individuality whatsoever—and so never seemed to particularly like me. She was holier-than-thou, showing up at all the religious festivals, annoying even the priest with her demanding ways. As Rinky mentioned her name, I saw her across the hall, holding on to the bride's sari and clutching the gifts that came the couple's way, having made herself the chaperone for the day. I couldn't imagine what she had to do with a big-time movie star.

"Madhu Sharma was called by Trixie Van Alden's assistant," Rinky continued. "It seems that Trixie was going to India anyway, and wanted to do something charitable, so Aunty Madhu suggested the mission. She was going to be in India for her wedding dress."

My head spun. I was riveted. Suddenly this whole conversation seemed so out of context. Ordinarily there would be no reason in the world why Rinky—or anyone here for that matter—would be talking about a major Hollywood star. But Trixie Van Alden and couture wedding gowns? This was a miracle.

I was salivating. I couldn't wait a second more to hear the rest.

"Apparently this actress has all these famous designers who want her to wear their dresses for her wedding, right? I'm sure you know all about that," Rinky said dismissively.

"But her assistant told Aunty Madhu that she heard about a village in India where the women sit for hours a day and do all the beading and embroidery for the big fashion brands and are paid practically nothing for it. So Trixie is going to go there directly and have a gown made, so these women will get all the publicity. And she's going to pay them what she would have paid for a dress from a fancy store. Aunty Madhu was very impressed. Of course, Trixie will take her own seamstress along. She's not going to trust some *darji* operating out of a shack, is she?"

Even as an ordinary reader and not the obsessed fashion/celebrity fan that I was, this was huge. It was the kind of thing I would love to read about in any magazine—how a big-name star was bucking convention, turning away from all the French couturiers and New York and Los Angeles designers who wanted to make her gown, and instead seek out something so unusual, so off the beaten track, in a remote village in India. In the world of celebrity news and fashion gossip, it didn't get much better than this.

My heart was beating so fast I thought I was going to faint.

Suddenly I had something that someone like Aaralyn Taylor would want. Sitting here innocently, a bystander at a wedding, I had stumbled across information that could make me invaluable to people in the media. Entertainment news shows, glossy magazines, supermarket tabloids:

They usually paid a fortune to get their hands on this kind of thing, and here, it had fallen into my lap. I knew for a fact that nobody else would have this information: I had read GossipAddict just this morning, and they updated their site almost every hour, and there was nothing on this.

I had butterflies in my stomach and felt a little giddy. But I had a sense I had never really felt before—as if everything were somehow within my reach. Despite what my father had said and the fact that I had a slightly odd-sounding name and was a marginally overweight dark-skinned girl from Agoura, a tiny voice in the back of my head told me I had what it took. Even that nebulous internship, which I had heard nothing about and the winner was to be announced in less than a month; there was, in my mind, no reason I couldn't have it.

Truth be told, by the end of my conversation with Rinky, I was feeling that there was no reason why I couldn't have anything.

While Rinky and I had been immersed in conversation, we had been swept up by the crowd and were now standing in front of the newlyweds. Aditya smelled of Old Spice, and his bride had way too much blush on. I stared at them, smiling, and hugged each one of them warmly and lovingly. I was suddenly feeling joyous, swept up on a wave of euphoria.

Suddenly my father was next to me.

"Come, let's eat," he said, leading me out of the crowd. "I know you have to go, but at least fill your stomach before you leave."

I accompanied my parents and my brother outside, where long tables had been set up holding large stainless steel containers of Indian food being warmed up by small burners underneath. I helped myself to *naan* bread and *bhindi masala*, to potatoes cooked with cumin seeds and thick yogurt mixed with crunchy cucumber and tomatoes. I was suddenly hungry and wanted to devour everything.

Before I knew it, it was one o'clock. I looked down at my outfit, realized I had no time to change, and like Cinderella after the ball, made a sprint for the main entrance of the temple, where I was told Aldo would be waiting. On my way out, I ran into Rinky again.

"Just wanted to say good-bye," I said, kissing her on the cheek. "I'll explain later. But I owe you one."

eighteen

Aldo didn't say anything to me, instead glancing for a minute at my shimmering silk and gold, most likely thinking how ridiculous I'd look and how clumsy I'd feel trying to chase after a two-year-old dressed like this. We coasted along the freeway in silence, just the gentle buzz of the radio in the background. It was another brilliant May day. The trees were rich and leafy, the sky a perfect shade of blue. And I was elated.

When we arrived, Juno let me in and while he tried to welcome me with warmth and enthusiasm, I could see the stress in his eyes.

"You look gorgeous, Indie," he said, gazing at my outfit. "Hope you didn't get all dressed up just for us," he laughed.

"I had a wedding to go to this morning and I meant to change before getting here but didn't have time," I explained before realizing that he wasn't really listening.

Kyle was sitting on the floor in the kitchen, playing with a remote-controlled car that beeped and lit up.

"Aaralyn usually doesn't like him playing downstairs—she thinks it makes the house look cluttered, but I tell her that's what children *do*," he said, a hint of frustration crossing his face. "But she's so preoccupied these days that I don't think she even notices."

He bent over to pick up his son, kissed him on the cheek, and handed him to me.

I heard the sound of tapping computer keys coming out of Aaralyn's office.

All the way over here, I was envisioning just how I was going to tell her what I had heard. I would be almost matter-of-fact about it, as if I stumbled across this kind of information every day. She would gaze at me with astonishment and intrigue. She would fling her arms around me, call up her contacts to verify the story—who of course wouldn't be able to deny it—and then thank me profusely. I was going to make her day.

But now that I was here, though, I wasn't quite sure when I would tell her. She was busy in her office and I had been summoned here to do nothing more than play with her child.

Juno disappeared into his clinic in the back. I got down on the carpet with Kyle and started building his blocks, and I waited.

"You look like you've just come off the set of a Bollywood movie," Aaralyn said, startling me.

I turned around. For someone who had been taking

lots of relaxing weekends off, she certainly didn't look very good. She had gray circles around her eyes, her hair was in a messy ponytail, and she was in sweatpants and a T-shirt. Even her fingernails, which I remembered so clearly from that first day I saw her because they were pointed and lilac and almost menacing in a pretty way, were now free of polish. They even looked like she had been chewing on them.

"Oh, I came straight from a wedding," I said, then explaining again what had happened to my change of clothes.

She looked me up and down, as if trying to figure out exactly what it was I was wearing. In the cool interior of her house, I felt rather garish and out of place.

"Well, you've got a few hours here this afternoon, and you need to be comfortable, so why don't you go upstairs and rifle through my closet? I have some stretchy pants I wore during my pregnancy that I've kept which might fit you. But take Kyle with you. I just came out to get some coffee, but need to go right back into my office."

Even though Aaralyn was suggesting that I could fit into her maternity clothes, I wasn't in the least bit offended. I was just so excited that I was going to be able to have an up close look in her closet. I had seen it from afar that first day here. But being given an all-access pass by one of the best-dressed women in America to wander through her wardrobe—what self-respecting fashion fiend wouldn't be *thrilled* at such a prospect?

I gathered up Kyle and some of his things and went upstairs, careful not to trip over my floor-sweeping *lehenga* in the process. Just as I was standing at the bottom of the steps about to go up, the doorbell rang. Nobody else appeared to answer it, so I stuck my eye to the peephole. Cayman was standing on the other side. I felt a little lurch in my stomach and opened the door.

He let out a long, low, soft whistle when he saw me.

"You look like a princess," he said.

I blushed.

"I was at a wedding," I repeated for the third time that hour.

"Well, no girl I know goes to weddings dressed like that. I'm impressed. It must have been some shindig."

"Actually, I was just about to go up and change. It's hard to run after Kyle with those gold threads prickling into my skin."

We both laughed.

I was beginning to like him more and more. And I hoped he felt the same way, although it was so hard to tell because he was always so genial. He was probably this nice and relaxed and charming with everybody. He was wearing an Levi's T-shirt and a leather cuff around his wrist. It took a seriously confident young guy to wear jewelry and still look masculine.

"I'm here to help Juno out again," he said, stepping in.

"He called last night, said he needed me for a few hours today. I was a bit bummed about it. Man, it's a gorgeous Sunday! And it's the last Sunday I'll be working for a while. Anyway, it's all good now." He looked straight at me and smiled again, his brown eyes softening even more.

"Well, I guess I'll see you later," he said, trying to make his way past my big froth of an outfit.

I nodded enthusiastically as Kyle kicked me in the thigh, telling me it was time to start moving.

All my friends were there. Chloé, Diane von Furstenberg, Oscar de la Renta. There was Michael Kors and Tommy Hilfiger and even a few hot new guys like Peter Som and Derek Lam. Not only was it the most gorgeous wardrobe I had ever seen, but it was also the most brilliantly organized. One section was all evening gowns, each one in a long transparent garment bag. Next to it was a grouping of semiformal cocktail dresses—Prada sheaths, some wispy Alberta Ferretti pieces. Another closet entirely held work and casual clothes; beautifully cut blazers from Giorgio Armani and tailored pants from Stella McCartney. And then her weekend clothes—a rundown of everybody from Escada Sport to Rock & Republic jeans, some of which still had four-hundred-dollar price tags stuck to them.

I had never been this close to such gorgeousness before. So immersed was I in the glamorous clothes in front of me that I almost forgot why I was here. Instead, I stood there, fingering a Carolina Herrera satin gown and staring closely at some tube beads on an ice-blue Badgley Mischka. I was almost about to start rifling through the three racks of shoes beneath—the Christian Louboutins and Stephane Kélians—when Aaralyn's voice sounded behind me.

"What *are* you doing?" she asked, holding her son. "Kyle was outside, at the top of the steps. Did you forget you had him in here with you? Good thing the gate was up so he couldn't go anywhere; he could have tumbled down the steps," she said.

"Crap," I said under my breath. "I'm really sorry, Aaralyn, I just got so caught up in your beautiful wardrobe. I've never seen anything like it. You really have the most incredible clothes."

"Thank you," she said tersely. "And you're really not going to find something to wear in *there*," she said, motioning to her closet. "I should have been more specific. Come here."

I followed her to a dresser against a wall, where she pulled open a drawer.

"Here," she said, pulling out some drawstring pants from the Gap and a long-sleeved cotton top. "I was about to give these to Goodwill. But I suppose you can have them, if you'd like. I think they'd suit you."

She tossed the clothes at me and put Kyle back on the

floor. This was my chance, I thought. I was alone in the room with her, had her full attention, and also probably needed to slightly redeem myself after she had found me rummaging through her closet like a burglar. I opened my mouth to say something. But the look on Aaralyn's face told me she had something better to do and couldn't wait to get back to her office. She turned around and left the room. I peeled off my ornate Indian clothes and shrugged into the clean and comfortable simplicity of Aaralyn's castoffs, and then went back downstairs to resume my duties.

But, hopefully, I'd soon get a chance to make Aaralyn happy first.

nineteen

The afternoon had gone smoothly enough. Although Kyle had refused to nap, at least he had played quietly and didn't even ask for his mother. I was keeping an eye on the back door, hoping that Cayman would appear again. But obviously Juno was keeping him busy in there. As Kyle fidgeted with some large multicolored magnets, I started thinking again about the juicy news I was sitting on, wondering when the timing might be right.

Suddenly I heard a loud bang from Aaralyn's office. I scooped Kyle up and ran in there. I remembered the place from my first day here. But today, it was in a state of total disarray. Papers were scattered all over the desk, and files were laid out over the emerald-green Persian rug on the floor. There was an upside-down slipper in one corner, a stained coffee mug on a side table. It looked as if she had been in here for hours. Even the room felt stressed.

"Aaralyn, is everything okay?" I called out.

The cordless phone was on the floor, smashed into six

pieces. Aaralyn had thrown it against the wall. Now, her head was in her hands and she looked like she was crying.

"What happened?" I asked her, instinctively putting my hand on her shoulder, before realizing that even that was completely out of line. I don't think I had ever touched her before.

"Nothing you would understand," she said, stomping out and shrugging my hand off her. A few minutes later, I heard her in the backyard, arguing with Juno. Cayman had come into the house, in an apparent bid to get away from them.

"What happened?" I asked him, genuinely alarmed. It was like someone had died.

"A car company that sponsored a couple of pages in the magazine every issue just pulled out. Didn't give a reason. Aaralyn is distraught. Juno is trying to calm her down, but I don't think it's working. He's going to give her some St. John's wort. She'd need a massive dose of it, though," he said.

Five minutes later, Aaralyn came back in, a little more composed. She poured herself a drink of water and told me she was going back into her office.

It was now or never, I said to myself.

I had access to some information that would, if nothing else, help turn around Aaralyn's day. There was no need for me to hang on to it anymore.

I asked Cayman to watch Kyle for a few minutes. He

looked at me quizzically when I told him I was going to talk to Aaralyn, but didn't ask me about it.

The door to her office was shut. I knocked softly on it and waited.

"Who is it?" she asked gruffly.

"It's me," I replied. "Indie."

"What do you want? I'm in the middle of something."

"I need to talk to you," I replied, trying to stop my voice from shaking. "It's important."

"If it's about Kyle, go ask his dad. I can't really deal with him right now."

"It's not about Kyle. It's about your magazine."

She opened the door and stepped aside to let me in.

"What is it?" she asked, her arms folded across her chest. "If you've come in here to blather on about how fabulous the magazine is, it's not a good time."

"It's about Trixie Van Alden," I replied, realizing how ridiculously out of context the words sounded. These were things that Aaralyn and I had never discussed.

"What about her?" she asked, a look of impatience on her face.

"You know there's all that talk about where she's getting her wedding dress?"

As I spoke, something inside me shifted. Suddenly I became more assertive and defined. There was a tone of maturity in my voice that even I had never noticed before. I was talking to Aaralyn as if I were her equal. I knew this feeling was fleeting and transient, but for now, it was all I had.

Then I launched right into the story, leaving out all the extraneous details about Rinky and Madhu Sharma, and going straight to the heart of the matter: that Hollywood's hottest star, who had French couture houses and renowned Italian designers begging her to wear one of their dresses, was heading to the villages of India to source a hand-beaded frock.

"Of course, she's taking her own seamstress," I said with a final flourish. "But the best part is—the craftswomen in India get paid directly, every dollar that they're worth."

Aaralyn was staring at me as if I had just told her that the world was about to self-destruct in eleven minutes.

"How do you know this?" she asked, a frown on her face.

"I can give you all my sources," I continued.

"Hang on a second," she said and went to her desk. She was about to pick up her phone until she saw the cordless handset, lying in a half dozen pieces, forlorn on the floor. So she reached into her handbag that sat on a couch, pulled out her cell phone, and punched in a few numbers.

"Meghan, hi, it's Aaralyn," she said. "I figured I'd find you in the office on a Sunday. Listen, I need you to check something out for me. It's about . . ."

She stopped, shut her eyes for a minute, and bit her lip. "Never mind," she said. "I'll take care of this."

As I watched, she sat down at her computer and pulled up her address book. There were hundreds of names and numbers. I was now standing right behind her and could read many of them. I saw her scroll down alphabetically past Selma Blair to Sandra Oh and Sharon Stone. Several more lines and she was at Trixie Van Alden, the name and number of her assistant right next to it.

This list must be worth gold, I thought to myself.

"Hi, Janna? It's Aaralyn Taylor," she said, a smile now on her face, her voice all charm and friendliness. Who could have imagined that just minutes earlier, this woman was in full meltdown mode?

"I'm great, thanks, how are you?" She paused, listening thoughtfully to the response, concentrating so much on the conversation that she didn't realize I was still standing there. Or maybe she didn't care. But because she hadn't dismissed me yet, I was standing firm. I wasn't going to miss this for anything.

"Oh, right, that film was shot in Bulgaria, wasn't it? That must have been quite a trip," she continued. "I saw in *Variety* that it's slated for an end-of-year release. Sounds like a good one."

She paused again.

"Listen, Janna, I'm sorry to ring you on a Sunday. I'm sure you get a million calls a minute about Trixie's wedding gown. So I'm not going to ask you the same questions. But I *am* just going to ask you to confirm or deny something. India. Calcutta. Hand-beading. Village damsels. A stop at a charity mission. Any of this sounding familiar?"

Aaralyn was now smiling sneakily. She was in her element. This seemed to be what she most loved doing—asking questions, soliciting answers.

"Oh really?" she asked. She turned around to look at me and arched an eyebrow. Then she did something that I didn't think I'd ever see Aaralyn do. She gave me a thumbs-up. Then she grabbed a pen and started scribbling down what Janna was telling her.

"Of course, it didn't come from you," she said. "And of course, we'll play it big. But I need you to make sure that nobody else gets the scoop on this, okay? You let us break the news—and I promise you I will write it myself—and I give you my word that when Trixie's new movie comes out, we'll give her the cover."

She nodded at Janna's response, smiled broadly, and put the phone down.

Then she stood up and turned around to face me.

I was waiting for the hug, for the big glorious "thank you," the slap on the back, the compliments. Almost instantaneously, my mind went to the summer that lay just at my doorstep, to the internship that would be naturally granted to me because, quite honestly, who else could possibly compete for it now? In my mind's eye, I could see everything unfolding so vividly after that; within a week of being an intern at Aaralyn's magazine, I would move swiftly up the ladder to become a staff writer. I would be the youngest fashion writer anywhere and would become the one that everyone wanted to talk to. Mediabistro.com would feature me as a wunderkind journalist. Everyone would know me as the girl who started out as a babysitter and who went on to land the hottest internship going. I would start getting offers from every other magazine, but would remain eternally loyal to Aaralyn. My star was about to rise. I could feel it.

But when I faced Aaralyn, she was just staring at me, the smile now completely gone from her face.

"How did you know this?" she asked, frowning. "How is it that I have paid insiders at all the best boutiques and fashion houses, and they couldn't get me this information, yet you pull it out of your hat? What do you know that I don't?"

Was she angry at me? I had just done her a huge favor, yet here she was, talking to me in this really accusing tone.

"Someone at the wedding this morning told me," I said, speaking softly. I recounted my conversation with Rinky, and how she was told something by someone close to an Indian charitable organization.

"I know it seems a bit roundabout, but as you see, it's all true."

She stared at me blankly, her head somewhere else. "Thanks," she said tersely. "You can go now."

I turned to walk out the door.

"Just a sec, Indie," Aaralyn said. This was it. This was going to be the big congratulatory expression of gratitude. And then she'd offer me the job. I knew she would.

"Kyle barely touched his lunch. Make sure he eats something, will you?"

twenty

Five days later, a brand-new issue of *Celebrity Style* was in our mailbox.

My first reaction was to throw it away.

Ordinarily, that would be sacrilege. After all, I had hoarded every copy of the last three years.

But after that last Sunday at Aaralyn's house, I wanted nothing more to do with her or the magazine.

I had not realized the extent of my bitterness until I saw the issue, the same one that contained a lead story on Trixie Van Alden, a story that Aaralyn wouldn't even have if it hadn't been for me.

When I had left her house that Sunday, she hadn't even said "thank you." She had paid me for babysitting Kyle, like she always did, and said she'd call me again if she needed my services. Then she had shut the door on me, leaving me to wait outside for my father to come and pick me up. I had stood there, wearing her hand-me-downs, carrying in my left hand a bag containing my glittery clothes from earlier. I had fought back tears because I didn't want my father to see me upset. But I felt hollow inside. I felt like I had been used.

Grudgingly, now, I took the magazine out of the mailbox with the rest of that day's delivery and went upstairs with it. I glanced at the cover as I treaded up the flight of steps: On the upper right-hand corner was a cropped picture of Trixie Van Alden. Underneath were the words: EXCLUSIVE TO CS: TRIXIE'S SECRET WEDDING DRESS REVEALED!

I was feeling so resentful, I had to read the story. Sitting on my bed, with a steaming-hot cup of cocoa and tiny white marshmallows bobbing around on top, I went straight to the contents section, saw what page the story was on and immediately leafed to it.

There was a full-length picture of Trixie across the page, and next to it a detailed story about the dress that she was going to wear at her upcoming wedding. The "source close to the star," I figured, must have been Janna. But there were numerous other people quoted, including Madhu Sharma. I guessed that Aaralyn must have been paying attention when I mentioned all these names to her. I thought of how Aunty Madhu must have felt, being called by an important magazine, and then seeing her name in print. Aaralyn had even tracked down a travel agent in Calcutta that was arranging Trixie's visit with her entourage. And there was even a photograph of a cluster of village women sitting in a thatched hut, surrounded by spindles and old-style weaving machines. A caption underneath said: NATIVE CRAFTSWOMEN AT WORK.

I closed my eyes for a minute and started to tell myself that I should feel proud. All along, for all these years, I had dreamed of one day being able to contribute to a publication like *Celebrity Style*. Now, I had actually done it; sure, it was in a roundabout way, and I certainly got no credit for it. But it was better than nothing.

But no matter how hard I tried to tell myself this, something inside still hurt. I realized then that giving Aaralyn the story was only half my objective that day; the rest was winning her approval. I thought one would give me the other. Obviously I was wrong. And the fact that I was wrong on something so elemental left me with a dull ache inside.

Almost obsessively, I turned back to the magazine. At the end of the feature, a small-print italicized line said: *MORE ON PAGE 60*. I flipped to that page and was astonished at what I saw there. It was a double-page spread on Indian-inspired clothing that had been worn by movie and television stars in the last few years: There was television actress Kelli Williams and British actress Helen Mirren both wearing *saris* at different awards shows and Cate Blanchett in rich gold Indian jewelry at the Oscars. There was a shot of Madonna in her *mehendi* and *bindis*, and pictures of Indian designer Ritu Beri, who shows her collections in Paris and dressed Nicole Kidman for the premiere of *Moulin Rouge*. There were photos of Judi Dench in an elegant embroidered tunic-and-pant set that could have come from Armani, but was instead from famous Indian design duo Abu-Sandeep. My heart swelled with pride. Right then, for me, it felt cool to be Indian.

That night, as my father and I sat in front of the television before dinner, I turned to *Access Hollywood*. There was a story that was basically a repeat of the piece in *Celebrity Style* on Trixie Van Alden. *Entertainment Weekly* and *The Insider* had done the same, as I gathered by all my flicking back and forth. They all cited *Celebrity Style* as having broken the news. I could just imagine Aaralyn, smug and self-satisfied, taking all the congratulations that were no doubt coming her way, not even giving me a second thought.

My father was half watching, not really paying attention, until he heard the name of the magazine, and of Aaralyn.

"That's your lady, nah?" he said, reclining against a dark red velvet cushion on the couch. "She's done well with this."

"Actually, Dad," I started. "I gave her that story."

He looked over at me, a puzzled expression on his face. I told him about that day at Aditya's wedding and my conversation with Rinky. All the while, my head was telling me to shut up, that I was telling him more than I needed to, that I was just giving him ammunition. But I wanted to prove to him that I knew vaguely what I was doing, even if I hadn't exactly gotten any credit for it.

"You know, a lot of magazines *pay* for that kind of information," he said. "These magazines need regular, ordinary people to feed them stories. Without assistants and waitresses and hairdressers, those pages would be empty. One of my patients was a concierge at a five-star hotel and used to call these gossip rags with information about movie stars. He would get hundreds of dollars in return."

"Which probably helped him pay *your* bills," I said under my breath. My father was right, which is why I was so upset with him. The odd thing was, I didn't want any money from Aaralyn. I knew that if I went to any other competing publication or TV news show, I probably could have lined my pockets with some cash. But I wasn't in it for that. I just wanted Aaralyn to take me seriously. And the fact that she hadn't, after what I had just done for her, made me feel stupid.

I got up and went into the kitchen, to see how dinner was progressing. I could smell one of my favorite meals, just about done, in the oven: chicken baked with water chestnuts, almonds, and peas. My mother made it extra rich with lots of cheese and milk and cream soup. No wonder it was so hard for me to lose weight in this house. The way I looked had never been an issue for my parents; to them, a few pounds extra here and there were "healthy." There were no gym memberships and complicated diet regimens. My parents believed only in fresh food and walks around the block a few evenings a week.

Now, my mother looked at me oddly.

"What?" I asked her, grabbing a glass out of a cabinet and pouring in some lemonade from the fridge.

"Indie, I just heard what your father said to you."

I shrugged my shoulders nonchalantly.

"Indie," my mother continued. I could tell by her tone that this was going to be one of her "serious conversations." We had them every so often, like when I was ten and my maternal grandmother was about to have an angioplasty, or a year later when an uncle came to stay with us because he was going through a divorce. Or, the worst of all, when I was twelve and my mother had taken it upon herself to explain the birds and the bees to me. She had asked me if we had "sex education" in school. I nodded, squirming, wanting desperately to change the subject. But she had decided to forge on, basically repeating everything I was learning at school, with the horrifyingly embarrassing addition of diagrams and illustrations that she had drawn herself. I had wanted to crawl under the table and die.

"What is it, Mom?" I asked, absentmindedly stirring the ice in my lemonade with my finger.

"Your father, he is right," she said quietly. "That Aaralyn, she doesn't respect you enough. She doesn't value you. Come, Indie, sit," she said, leading me to the breakfast nook in the kitchen. I didn't want to go with her, but knew I had to.

"Look, Mom, I was in the middle of watching something," I said. I knew this conversation was going to be uncomfortable and I hated discomfort.

"Just give me a minute of your time, Indie," she said, her voice quiet. "I don't ask much of you. I just need you to listen to me now."

I put my glass of lemonade down, letting the condensation that had formed outside drip onto the table. My mother handed me a coaster.

"That day, years ago, when you found that book on fashion in the library. Remember? Indie, I was so happy that day. Finally I thought you had come across something that really interested you. I have always been very proud of you for not abandoning it, for not letting it become just another whim and fancy. Other kids had their momentary indulgences: skateboards and magic tricks and pets that they once loved but soon got bored with. But you, Indie, you were never like that with your interest in fashion. You loved it then, and you love it still. And that tells me you will most likely always love it."

As I sat here at this table, across from my mother, what gladdened my heart the most was that she had actually seen me all these years. Even when she was quiet and in the background of my young life, she was still a witness to it.

"But all this, now, with this lady, it hurts me so," she said. "I know you enjoy being there, looking after her child. I know you feel you are fulfilling some destiny. Ordinarily, Indie, I would be behind you with that. I have always wanted you not just to excel, but to be happy. To thrive in life. But when I see someone not appreciating you the way you should be appreciated—Indie, that breaks my heart. You are my precious daughter, my firstborn. I want all of life's good things to come to you. But at the very top of that list is the consideration of other people. I don't care that Aaralyn is famous and wealthy and successful. I care only that she is a kind and decent human being. And no kind and decent human being would stand by and watch a sixteen-year-old girl's dreams be crushed if they could do something about it.

"If I know one thing, Indie, it is this," my mother continued. "Whatever it is you set your mind on, you will succeed at. You are a tremendous student, gifted in every way. We are proud to have a daughter like you. But my first instinct as your mother is to protect you. And until Aaralyn begins to respect your value to her, well, Indie, I don't think I want you to work there anymore."

. . .

I couldn't forget my mother's words even weeks after that night. June had just begun, and in ten days, school would be out and the magazine would notify whoever it was that had won the internship.

Instinctively, I knew it wasn't me. I had barely been in touch with Aaralyn and even on those days I had gone over to babysit Kyle, the subject had never come up.

Getting it now would be a miracle.

But I didn't want to think about it anymore. I was determined to enjoy the glorious weather and all it brought. I wanted to be a teenager again, spending time with Kim whenever she wasn't with Brett. The school's newspaper, which I had occasionally contributed to in the past, had asked me to help put together an end-of-year issue, with lots of fun projections about what students were going to do with their summer. There was drama club and choir practice. I was a busy, involved student.

Kim and I were sampling sliced apricots and gourmet olives at the Farmer's Market in Calabasas one Saturday morning. I loved it here. Everyone was always so cheerful, so happy to be close to food. I couldn't really afford to buy very much except a homemade quiche and maybe an apple. But on this one particular Saturday, Kim was telling me that Tyler and Brooke had finally become an item, that she had started taking his calls after that run-in at Cold Stone Creamery.

"But Tyler keeps telling Brett about how Brooke is so obsessed with that fashion magazine internship, you know, the one you were after," said Kim, spearing a toothpick into a cube of cheese laid out on a sample platter. "It's making Tyler crazy because it's all Brooke talks about. Seems that Aaralyn is having a hard time with her kid," Kim recounted, third-hand. "They even went to a child psychologist, who said Kyle needed more attention from his parents. So Aaralyn has to spend more time at home with her son on weekends. Maybe that's why you haven't heard from her."

"Oh, and there's something else," Kim said. "An Italian publisher wants to buy *Celebrity Style*."

I almost choked on the chocolate-covered strawberries we were now trying.

"Brooke was going on about what would happen if the magazine was sold. It'll make Aaralyn a lot of money, *and* she'll get to stay on as editor."

Two days later, as I was scrolling through Monster.com to see if there were any summer opportunities for fashion-obsessed sixteen-year-olds (there weren't), my mother knocked on the door and told me Aaralyn Taylor was on the phone. She had a stoic, almost stern look on her face.

"Are you sure you want to talk to her?" my mother asked as I started making my way down the stairs. "Remember, you are not the puppet she wants you to be."

"Mom, chill. It's probably nothing," I said, my heart beating fast. Maybe Aaralyn had finally come to her senses and wanted to thank me properly for the Trixie Van Alden exclusive. Maybe Juno had weighed in on how downright rude she had been and that she owed me more than my babysitting money. I was curious to find out, but held out no expectations.

"Hello?" I said into the receiver.

"Indie, hello." Aaralyn sounded very businesslike. "How are you?"

Then, without waiting for an answer, she asked me another question.

"Do you have a passport?"

After Paris, Milan was the second place in the world I had always wanted to visit.

I couldn't believe that Aaralyn Taylor had invited me to accompany her. Her weekday nanny couldn't travel and Juno had a conference to attend in Oregon. So Aaralyn had to take Kyle along to some very important meetings and needed someone to come along and watch him while she conducted her business.

"It'll be the week that school is out," she said. "That way, you won't miss anything. It'll just be a few days. I'm happy to ask your parents for permission. It would be harder for them to say no to me than to you."

I had told Aaralyn that I'd call her back after I had

spoken to my parents. I already knew what they were going to say and could understand why. But realistically, how could I possibly say no? Granted, I had almost written Aaralyn Taylor off, figuring I would probably never hear from her again after she had taken what she needed from me.

But I didn't see this as having anything to do with Aaralyn Taylor. This was about seeing Milan. It was about an opportunity that I would probably never have again.

My parents, not surprisingly, didn't quite share my enthusiasm.

"Milan? You mean in Italy? In Europe?" my father asked, flabbergasted that I could even consider it. "Alone?"

"Dad, I'm not alone. I'm with Aaralyn. She knows the city inside out." I said, starting to feel desperate. I was still a minor. They could still say no.

"We know nothing of this woman," my father said, my mother standing resolutely by his side. "I'm presuming she will be leaving you alone in the hotel with that child of hers as she goes off and does her business. I'm not comfortable with that at all. Anything could happen to you. You are still our responsibility, Indie." His eyes were stern and resolute. Mine, however, were starting to fill with tears. Seeing that, his voice softened.

"I suppose, if you really wish to go, Mummy can

accompany you as a chaperone," he said. "I have miles. I can get her a ticket. She can share your hotel room. Of course, we'll have to get her a visa. Those Indian passports, you need a visa to go to the toilet."

"*Dad!* I'm supposed to be going to babysit a kid and now you want mom to babysit me? That's *beyond* embarrassing!"

"Indie, I don't see another way. I have been very accepting of your choices up until now, but I don't know these people. And from what I have seen so far, I am not very impressed with them. You know, most Indian parents would never allow such a thing. Mohit keeps his girls under lock and key. I am trying to be modern. But I am still an Indian father after all. In Calcutta, a girl your age wouldn't be able to go to the next town by herself, much less another continent."

"Dad, I'm not in Calcutta," I said, tears now streaming down my cheeks. I was shaking. I was genuinely scared that my father would put his foot down and stamp out my dream to go to Italy. I wanted to yell and scream and run upstairs and lock the door. But I knew that if I behaved like that, I definitely would not be allowed to go. So I took a deep breath, lowered my voice, and wiped away my tears.

"Please, Dad," I begged. "You don't know how important this is to me. Look," I said, my mind now racing ahead, desperation overcoming me. "If you allow me to go, when I get back, I'll go to India with Uncle

Mohit's daughters. I promise. And I'll stop with all this fashion thing. Things will really change around here. I'll be the kind of daughter you wanted." I had started sobbing again.

My father stood up, came to me, and put his arm around me.

"You're a good girl, Indie," he said softly. "I just wish you were a little more *serious*, that's all." He paused. Then he said, "Get this Aaralyn woman on the phone."

twenty-one

The last day of school before summer was usually the best day of the year. Better than my birthday. Better than Christmas. The whole week leading up to it was a write-off, although the teachers pretended it wasn't. But the halls were abuzz with excitement. Nobody paid attention to what was going on in class. All sorts of things were let slide. There was no homework. The last day of the semester before summer break was filled with promise—of memorable and fun times ahead. Everyone talked excitedly about their plans and smiled through even the dreariest lessons. Everyone was more casual than usual; flip-flops, faded T-shirts, clam-diggers. Everyone was happy. The stress of the prom—which I hadn't gone to because nobody had asked me—and putting out the yearbook was over. Spring was in the air and everyone smiled.

I smiled more, because in a week I was going to Italy.

When my father had gotten on the phone with Aaralyn that day, I had snuck upstairs and picked up the extension. I'm certain they both knew I was listening in, but neither one of them seemed to mind.

"I can completely understand your concerns," she had said to him. "As a parent, I'm certain I would have the same reservations. But I can assure you that I will look after her as if she were my own. She's a wonderful companion for Kyle. I cannot tell you how much I would appreciate your permission."

"Okay," my father said, a tone of reluctance still in his voice. "My Indie speaks very highly of you and your family. So I am entrusting her safety and well-being to you."

I was jubilant. I had never been so ecstatic. Milan with Aaralyn Taylor—it was like my prayers had been answered.

On the last day of school, I could think of nothing else. Whenever a friend or teacher asked me what my plans were, I couldn't conceal my excitement, blurting out that I was being taken to Italy as a babysitter. Mr. Baker and Ms. Jennings, who had planned the career day when I had first met Aaralyn Taylor, were especially impressed, particularly after I told them how I had come to be Kyle's babysitter to begin with. Even Mr. Fogerty, who had always rolled my eyes at my apparently frivolous ways, now looked at me with a new admiration.

"Well, that was very enterprising of you," Ms. Jennings said, when I recounted how I had literally run after Aaralyn's departing car. "I wouldn't have thought you had that in you."

All day, I felt like I was walking on a marshmallow cloud. I felt invincible and confident and a little bit like a grown-up.

But then, along came Brooke.

Since our last exchange some weeks ago when she had mocked the fact that I was babysitting her cousin, she had virtually ignored me. It was like she had gone from not even noticing me to looking down on me.

But a few hours before the end of school, while I was retrieving something from my locker, Brooke came up behind me and tugged the strap on my shoulder bag.

"Hey, suck-up face," she said. I turned around. She had a sneer on her face, a cold anger in her eyes.

"What did you call me?" I said, frowning. I might have been occasionally shy, but I was not a doormat.

"Suck-up face," she said, her words ugly compared to the prettiness of her face. "You have a problem with that?"

"I think *you're* the one with the problem," I said.

She stared at me through glassy blue eyes. "I'm going to see to it that you don't get to go to Italy," she hissed. I was completely taken aback. I hadn't thought that she would even care. Brooke Carlyle was one of those girls who traveled frequently, whose parents took her to the British Virgin Islands in summer and Aspen for Christmas. She spent long weekends at spa resorts with her mother, who I had learned was Aaralyn's older sister. If Brooke ever wanted to go to Italy, all she would have had to have done was mention it to her venture capitalist father, and a ticket would have been waiting on her dresser by the end of the day.

"What's the problem?" I asked. "Your aunt asked me to help her out. It has nothing to do with you."

"That's where you're mistaken," she said. "My aunt totally wants me to go. She even called me before she called you. But by the time I got back to her, you had already thrown yourself at her."

"I don't know what you're talking about," I said, growing irritated. "It doesn't matter who she called first. What matters is what she's decided—and she wants to take me. Now, if you don't mind, I have a class to get to," I said, slamming my locker door shut and squeezing past her.

I was uneasy the rest of the day. Brooke Carlyle was not a girl to be trifled with. She had clout among the "in" crowd at school, and brains, money, and looks—a lethal combination in anyone and never more so than in a sixteen-year-old girl who thrived on competition. What if she *was* trying to convince Aaralyn to take her instead of me? I would be devastated. I had never looked forward to anything this much in my whole life. And, based on the promise I had made to my father, this was going to be my last hurrah—my final exposure to the world of fashion and everything I loved about it, before giving it all up, buckling down to my studies and focusing on something much more sensible for the rest of high school. When the fall semester started, it would be time for me to start bonding with my slide rule and stop spending hours a day reading GossipAddict.com, which, as it turned out, I had become addicted to.

When I got home that afternoon, there was a message from Aaralyn. I felt sick to my stomach. Brooke had probably gotten to her and had somehow convinced her to take her instead of me. I burst into tears, while my mother looked at me in dismay.

"Just call Aaralyn back," my mother said. "You don't know what she wanted. And really, Indie, she doesn't seem like the kind of woman who would ask you to commit to something and then change her mind suddenly."

"Maybe not," I said. "But you don't know Brooke. That girl has a way of getting everything she wants."

When I got Aaralyn on the phone, which wasn't until late that evening at home, she sounded like she had almost forgotten why she had called.

"Oh yes, right," she said, her mind obviously someplace else. "I just wanted to remind you to travel light. I plan on shopping there and will need some of your luggage allowance."

I let out a huge sigh of relief. But I still wanted to ask Aaralyn about Brooke. We had never talked about her niece before, but after what had happened today, there was a part of me that wanted to know where I stood.

"Aaralyn, just one other thing," I said. "Brooke came up to me at school today and told me that you had originally asked her to come with you and babysit, and that I was your second choice. That's okay if it's true. But she seemed really upset about the whole thing and was not very pleasant to me."

There was a momentary silence on the other end of the line.

"I really don't have the time to get involved in your silly schoolgirl squabbles," said Aaralyn tersely. "Just be ready by five p.m.," she said. "I'll send Aldo for you."

twenty-two

In the few days leading up to my departure, I must have tried on every single piece of clothing in my closet, in almost every possible permutation. I had checked on weather.com and found out that it was sunny and warm, which meant that I could choose from my lightest and prettiest LA clothes.

But I was going to Milan, a city known for its incredibly stylish women, and all of a sudden my floaty skirts with their beaded borders and jersey halter tops and capri pants and embroidered flip-flops looked dated. But given that my parents refused to buy me any extra clothes, I had no choice but to take whatever I had.

The night before we were scheduled to leave, I was up packing until two a.m. I planned for between two and three outfits a day—didn't people in Europe change for dinner?—as well as a couple of jackets in case the weather changed. I pulled out my favorite cosmetics—my Juicy Tubes lip glosses and Wet 'n' Wild eye pencils—and packed each one in little sandwich bags, so nothing would spill. I took my Maybelline body shimmer and three Mary Kay nail polishes that my mother had bought from our next-door neighbor, and wrapped them carefully in a small toiletries pouch. I packed a pair of espadrilles, some Skechers, some wedges. Because I knew I needed both hands free for Kyle, I packed a slouchy metallic leather knapsack that would carry all his snacks and toys.

Then I closed and locked the suitcase, left my carry-on bag open for my last-minute toiletries and magazines, and prepared myself for a night during which I knew I'd be far too excited to sleep.

Aldo was waiting for me early. Even though I was already packed, there had still been a mountain of things to take care of today, and I still wasn't ready when he got here. I had spent a couple of hours getting my hair and nails done, had gone to get my arms and legs waxed and my eyebrows threaded, and had made a quick stop at the dry cleaners to pick up a silk cami that I couldn't imagine *not* having during my first-ever trip to Italy.

Just as I was lugging my bag downstairs, my mother summoned me. I left my suitcase by the door and went to find her. She was seated on the carpeted floor of a spare linen closet that she had converted into a miniature temple.

"Come here," she said, pulling me by the hand. I squeezed on the floor next to her. I so rarely came in here.

I looked around at all the photographs on the wall and lined up on tiny shelves; Durga and Krishna, Ganesh and Laxmi, their beatific faces and brightly colored clothes, all of them holding conches or tridents, eyes half closed, palms facing outward in blessing. My parents came in here every morning after they had bathed, and last thing at night before going to bed. I, however, only entered right before we were all going on our trips to India, in what I had always perceived as a last-minute bid to make sure we wouldn't all perish in some horrific airline crash.

"Cover your head," my mother instructed me. I reached into a small lacquered box that was filled with scarves, pulled one out, and placed it on top of my head.

My mother closed her eyes and folded her hands together, whispering strange Sanskrit words under her breath. I knew she was praying for me—that not only would I come home safely from my first-ever trip away from home without my parents, but that I would be shielded from anything unfavorable or dangerous while I was in a strange land. She separated her hands and placed them both over a small flame that she had lit before starting her prayers, and then placed her hands on my head in a show of blessings.

"There. Now you are protected," she said.

It was hard for me not to cry.

The doorbell rang and I told my mother that I had to go. I had already said good-bye to my father that morning;

he had a scheduled surgery in the afternoon, so he wouldn't make it home in time to see me off. Dinesh came bounding downstairs, threw one arm around my waist, lightly pressed his head to my stomach, and said, "Bye, sis, have a good time," before turning around and running back up to his room.

My mother turned to me, pulled me close toward her, and started crying. "Bye, my *beti*, stay safe, God be with you," she said, crying into my shoulder.

"Mom, come on. I'm not being deployed to Iraq," I said, trying to steady my own voice. "I'll be home before you know it. I'll call when we land, I promise."

We were going to pick up Aaralyn next.

When we got there, she was already waiting outside, Juno holding Kyle. I saw another figure next to them; it was Cayman. It had been weeks since I'd last seen him, which had been that day when I had given Aaralyn the Trixie Van Alden scoop. But the fact that I hadn't seen him recently, combined with the fact that that whole day was unpleasant in how I was treated, had made Cayman fade into the back of my mind.

But seeing him now, standing next to the Taylor family, the sun brightening his ash-blond hair, a slight breeze blousing up his salmon-colored shirt—he looked so appealing that the sight of him now thrilled me a little.

We pulled to a stop. Juno lifted up the car seat that was

on the sidewalk next to him and clicked it into place in the limo, buckling Kyle in and kissing him good-bye.

Aaralyn got in without addressing Aldo and just glared at him for being eight minutes late. She waited as Aldo loaded her two Louis Vuitton cases into the trunk, saying nothing to me except a curt "hi."

"Crap, I forgot my phone," she said, rummaging through her bag.

"I'll run in and get it," I offered, Aaralyn yelling out that she'd left it charging in her office.

"I'll come with," Cayman said, following me inside the house.

"You must be really excited," Cayman said as we walked in through the front door, which had been left ajar. "Milan on someone else's dime. Can't beat that."

"I'm just the babysitter," I said, suddenly more aware of the reason I was going.

We were in Aaralyn's darkened office. I saw her cell on a table in the corner and yanked the cord out of the wall socket with the phone still attached. I turned around to head back out, and Cayman was standing right in front of me.

"I was hoping I'd see you before you left," he said, his voice now low.

My heart was beating so fast I thought I was going to faint. He smelled faintly of leather polish and ginger. When I had first met him, I had dreamed about a moment like this. But now that I was here, and it was real, I didn't have a clue what to do.

"I won't be here when you get back," he said. "I'm going to spend a couple of months as a counselor at an outdoor adventure kids' camp in Santa Cruz. Rock-climbing, surfing, wilderness survival—all the stuff I love."

"Sounds great," I said, feeling self-conscious and disappointed at the same time.

Aldo honked the horn.

"I'd better get going," I said, trying to step around him, feeling curiously nervous.

"Wait," he said gently. "I've been thinking of you these past weeks." He came closer to me. I was suddenly conscious of what I must smell like; in retrospect, that cheese and onion on a toasted baguette that my mother had stuffed down my throat for lunch was a bad idea. I inhaled deeply, figuring that if I held my breath surely he wouldn't be able to detect it?

He reached out and put a hand on my shoulder in a move that felt a little awkward. I wasn't sure if he was going to hug me or wrestle me to the ground. He let his hand slide down my arm, where it rested on my hand, gently playing with my fingers.

"You're so different from all the other girls I meet," he said. "You're, well, really authentic. What you see is what you get. You're not that typical LA clone—you know, all skinny and pretentious. You have such a happy warmth to you."

My palms had started to sweat and the butterflies were flitting about wildly in my stomach. For a millisecond, my mind flashed to a scene from one of the first Bollywood films I'd ever watched, where the hero scooped up the heroine on their wedding night, carried her onto their rose petal–strewn nuptial bed, and came in for the big kiss. The camera had faded to black, leaving me to imagine what might have happened.

Cayman was suddenly so close to me that I could smell the vetiver coming off his freshly shaved skin. He was slightly bowed over me, so much so that at one point, the top of my head was right up against his chin. There, in the darkness of the room, as three impatient people and a baby waited outside, Cayman put his lips over mine. It felt so soft that I thought for a minute that a butterfly had escaped from my stomach and had landed on my mouth.

In the car, as Aaralyn got on the phone, I gave Kyle a packet of Wikki Stix to play with so he could be happily occupied. I wanted to replay what had just happened with Cayman, as if doing so would make it more real, because it felt like a dream.

I closed my eyes and remembered how his lips traveled from my mouth to my cheek, and how he lifted up my hand and kissed that too.

Now, I stared down at that hand, covering it protectively with the other one.

We had both left the house together and he had helped me into the car without saying much. He simply smiled at me, wished me a happy and safe trip, kissed me again chastely on the cheek, and waved us off with a casual, "See ya!" I wasn't sure what any of it meant, had had absolutely no experience in that area. But I didn't want to think about it. I just wanted to savor the moment.

"Meghan, I can't believe it's happened again," said Aaralyn, yelling so loudly that I was forced to stop daydreaming. "*Going For Broke* was *my* exclusive! How the hell did those idiots at GossipAddict get it?"

Her face was stony as Meghan said something, obviously to no effect.

Just that afternoon, I had seen the GossipAddict story on *Going For Broke*. It was supposed to be a romantic comedy that was going to open in a few weeks, and that everybody had been talking about because the producers were spending more money on costumes for this film than had been spent on any movie in decades.

Interestingly, it wasn't even a period piece; it wasn't as if they needed to hire someone to research eighteenth-century kimonos or Victorian English ball gowns. This was a contemporary movie, set in modern times, about a gorgeous but poor girl who has to decide if she will marry for love or money. The actress was Savannah Princeton, who regularly made Mr. Blackwell's Best Dressed List and was known as much for her sense of style as her Oscar-winning abilities.

The movie had been in the news because, instead of relying on borrowed props or loaned designer dresses, the executives behind *Going For Broke* had decided to buy extravagant couture gowns from Balenciaga and Chanel.

But what most people didn't know—and which GossipAddict.com had revealed for the first time—was that Savannah Princeton was behind that decision and had every intention of keeping everything she would wear in the film.

According to GossipAddict, there would be chinchilla coats and python-skin boots, French hand-beaded organdy gowns and Persian lamb jackets, Chopard dancing diamonds and Franck Mueller watches. She wanted an all-designer, all-original wardrobe, and had ignored the studio executives who told her that nobody in the audience would notice if a ring was an authentic Neil Lane or not. Gossipaddict had quoted a source close to the actress as saying she didn't want to be "obligated" to any fashion label, which is why she wanted everything she was to wear in the film to be purchased. The studio executives had sputtered, the gossip vultures were swirling, but Savannah Princeton was in an ironclad contract and the producers had to give in. She was the worst kind of Hollywood diva, the antithesis of someone like Trixie Van Alden, who had wanted the less fortunate to benefit from the excesses of the playground these people frolicked in. But Savannah Princeton—she was the kind of woman who was only in it for herself.

It had been a gripping little news feature—and one that was obviously meant for *Celebrity Style*.

"I need to find out how they're doing this," Aaralyn said, still on the phone with Meghan. "It's getting infuriating, and I'm not going to tolerate it anymore. Now we need to change next week's lineup. What have we got?"

She had a notebook in an Hermès binder on her lap, and was scribbling away with a pen, her ear glued to the phone. She tossed out names: Naomi Watts, Penelope Cruz, Jewel. What were any of them doing fashion-wise? Any style stories that could be rehashed? Had any of the staff writers got anything up their sleeves?

"The timing of this couldn't be worse," said Aaralyn to Meghan, as we continued on the 405. "If I want this sale to go through, these Italians need to be wowed by the magazine. The past few weeks have been decidedly underwhelming, and just when I thought I could pull a rabbit out of my hat with the Savannah Princeton story, along comes GossipAddict again. I can't afford to lose another story to them."

She nodded, squeezed shut her eyes, bit her lip, said good-bye, and hung up. She stared straight ahead, ignoring Kyle's whimpers, and mostly ignoring me, until we got to the airport.

. . .

Based on the lines in front of the Alitalia check-in counters at LAX, it was going to be a full flight. But Aaralyn, a Skycaps porter behind her, Kyle and I trailing him, strolled right to the red carpet in front of the first-class counter, brandishing her and Kyle's passports. She asked me for mine and plopped all three of them down in front of the airline employee.

I had never stood in the first-class line before and it gave me a little thrill. I looked over at the economy section, where dozens of people waited in a line that moved excruciatingly slowly. I had lots of experience in that line, standing there with my parents for sometimes two hours or more.

But this, with Aaralyn, was a whole other ball game. A small vase of fresh flowers was on the counter, the girl behind it smiling and polite, asking us about any special meal requests and if we would like to use the lounge. As I stood there, I recalled an interview I had read with a celebrity nanny—someone who had worked for a few megastars—who said that once you were in that league, you lived like your employers. This girl traveled by private jet with the family that she worked for and always stayed in a similar suite at the same five-star hotels they were at. She basically lived a movie star's life.

There could be worse jobs, I thought to myself, smiling as I imagined what it would be like to sink into a first-class seat, to eat proper food instead of a sandwich made from stale bread and wilted lettuce, to have a proper duvet blanket instead of those cheap acrylic ones they handed out in economy. I would put Kyle to sleep in his seat and turn on the personal DVD player that every passenger had. For once, I almost couldn't wait to get on the plane.

Aaralyn took the three boarding passes that the ticketing agent handed her and stuffed them into the outside pocket of her crocodile-skin bag.

"I'll hang on to your passport as well," she said, as we marched through security. "It'll be easier. You just look after Kyle."

We made our way to the first- and business-class lounge, where Aaralyn continued making phone calls while I ran after Kyle, who had squirted juice all over himself. I had been eyeing the snacks being offered, but seeing as Aaralyn wasn't eating and I was so preoccupied with Kyle, I elected to forego having anything; a first-class dinner would probably be much more delicious anyway.

Our flight was finally announced and I excitedly accompanied Aaralyn to the gate, saddled down with Kyle's diaper bag and activity pouch. They let us get on the plane first, and we strolled down the cool, quiet walkway, well ahead of most of the other passengers.

As soon as we were on the plane, Aaralyn was warmly greeted by the flight attendant, who offered to take her carry-on bag and lightweight coat. She glanced at the boarding passes and asked Aaralyn to follow her, and I traipsed along behind them. Aaralyn turned around and said, "Indie, you're back there." She was glancing beyond the curtain that separated first class from everything else behind it.

"Oh," I said.

"Yes, you and Kyle." Then she lowered her voice. "People who travel in the front of the plane don't generally like having kids close to them. Someone will show you to your seats. Just make yourselves comfortable, and I'll come check on you in a little while."

I was beyond embarrassed. What had given me the idea that Aaralyn would buy me a ticket to sit close to her?

The economy cabin was still relatively empty, only now slowly filling up with other families with children. Another flight attendant showed us our seats. At least I was next to the window. I got Kyle settled, buckled him in, and tried to relax. It was all going to be fine, I said to myself. I was still going to Italy.

As we prepared for takeoff, Kyle decided that he wanted to play hide-and-seek underneath the seats and started screaming when I told him he couldn't. Everyone turned to look at me, as if I was the lax mother who couldn't keep her child quiet. Kyle continued squirming and fussing in his seat, kicking the knee of a large-set man on the other side of him, who then asked the flight attendant if he could move. Everything I gave to Kyle to distract him ended him on the floor, embedded in the seat cushion, or up his nose.

As Kyle squirmed on my lap, I rummaged around in my bag to see if there was something in there I could distract him with—some keys, my cell phone, anything. At the bottom of the bag, I felt a small plastic bottle. Puzzled, I pulled it out. It was a clear container filled with golden liquid. There was a note attached to it that read, MY DEAR INDIE, THIS IS SOMETHING I USED ALL THE TIME ON YOU AND DINESH WHEN YOU WERE BABIES. JUST IN CASE YOU HAVE SOME NEED FOR IT WITH THE CHILD IN YOUR CARE, HERE IT IS. LOVE, MUMMY.

I turned the bottle around and read the ingredients: sweet almond, basil, rose, nutmeg. I opened the top and took a whiff, and was automatically transported back to my own childhood; the cool, clammy feel of the oil, its heady aroma, being cuddled in my mother's arms as she rubbed it on me.

I lay Kyle across my lap, dripped a few drops of the oil onto my fingers, and gently began massaging it into his forehead and behind his ears. As I did so, I sang to him, smiled at him, looked him right in the eyes, just as my mother had done with Dinesh and me.

Within twenty minutes he was asleep. Just as I was laying him down on his seat, Aaralyn came by. She had changed into pajamas that had been given to her on the plane and she looked enviably comfortable.

"Wow, he's out," she said.

"Yes," I whispered.

"Well done, Indie," she said, before turning around to go back to her rarefied cabin.

Finally. An accolade.

We didn't see her again until we were close to landing. She emerged through the curtains and I almost didn't recognize her. Her face was free of makeup, and without her usual sheer foundations and pretty pink blusher she looked pale and almost sick. Her hair was in a scrunchy. She had changed into a velour sweatsuit that made her look, well, *ordinary*. She was holding a glass of champagne, but looked like she had had enough to drink.

"We're almost there," she said. "Just get his things together and I'll meet you outside the plane."

In the arrivals terminal, I noticed people looking at us curiously, almost as if they were wondering what the connection was between us. There was Aaralyn, still looking grim and miserable, an exhausted suburban housewife instead of a glamorous fashion executive. She obviously didn't travel very well. She reminded me of all those pictures I would see in the celebrity magazines, taken by paparazzi staked out at international airports, of stars at their worst after a long flight. I supposed it didn't matter who you were—jet lag and dehydration happened to everyone.

But I had managed to look after myself a little better. I had spritzed my face with an essential oil spray that I had bought, meant just for air travel. Before we had landed, I had reapplied my makeup, wet and combed my hair, and straightened up my clothes. I had even cleaned up Kyle, who was now alert after several hours' sleep.

As we waited for our luggage, I looked after Kyle while Aaralyn fumed about having to pull her luggage off the conveyer belt herself. I watched, mildly amused, as she tried to lug her Vuitton case off, breaking a nail in the process, and swearing beneath her breath.

"Your babysitter seems to be having a bad day," said an American woman behind me, who had been staring at us in the immigration line.

"Excuse me?" I said.

"Your maid. She looks exhausted. Oh, and is this your brother? He is so cute," she continued, looking at Kyle. That she could even have assumed such a thing struck me as ridiculous; I was dark-skinned with black hair. Kyle was fair-skinned with red hair.

Or maybe she just assumed that one of us had been adopted.

I was about to correct her, but decided to let her have her delusions. This was the most fun I'd had since leaving Los Angeles. Given the way I had been treated by Aaralyn so far, I didn't feel very guilty having some fun at her expense.

 201

twenty-three

Even though it was night and the streets were dark, I couldn't take my eyes off the window.

Our driver, who had been waiting for us, holding a big placard with Aaralyn's name on it, told us that the traffic was free-flowing and we would be at our hotel in no time.

I didn't care how long it took. I was mesmerized by this place, by the bright orange trams that ran up and down the streets, the parks with their bronze statues and wet benches, the little cafés with their *al fresco* areas closed for the night, although people still milled about inside. It had been raining, but it was a warm evening, and I was thrilled to be there.

We pulled up outside the Grand Hotel. It was all lit up on the outside, a thick red mat at the front of the brass-framed glass doors. It looked spectacular. I waited for Aaralyn to tell me to stay in the car; after the airplane incident, I wouldn't have been surprised if she was sending me off to the Milan equivalent of the YWCA.

Thankfully, though, she left the door open for me, tipped the driver, instructed a doorman to bring in our luggage, and walked in. She marched straight to reception where she was greeted with a hug by the concierge, who remarked how long it had been since she had last been there.

"Not since the February shows, yes?" he asked.

I was totally impressed.

He held two keys, which relieved me to no end. While standing at reception I had even considered the possibility that Aaralyn would make me sleep on the floor of her room.

"The Giuseppe Verdi suite, your usual, is ready for you," the concierge said, leading us to the elevator. "And something nice for your assistant," he continued, looking at me.

So not a broom closet then, I thought to myself.

We went to Aaralyn's room first, which was about the plushest thing I had ever seen in my life; it was huge and filled with overstuffed silk couches and dark mahogany furniture. It was like something out of a palace.

"Go put your things down in your room and then come back here and get Kyle bathed and ready for bed," Aaralyn instructed me. "Try and get him to sleep, although it might take a few hours because he's so jet-lagged. Just deal with it. I need to get some rest."

I wanted to say something to her. I thought I was done

for the night, that I could go and take a bath and relax and see if this hotel had MTV on offer. I had been looking after Kyle for fourteen hours and deserved a break. I had barely slept on the plane, crammed into that tiny seat, as Aaralyn had luxuriated in what was basically a full-length bed.

"Actually, Aaralyn, I'm really, really tired," I said, my voice trembling. "Wouldn't you like to spend some time with Kyle? I'm sure he'd love it?" I continued brightly as Kyle lay wide awake facedown on the carpet. I bent down to pick him up.

"I have some important meetings tomorrow and need to be at my best," Aaralyn replied, unmoved. "You know, Indie, I brought you here for a reason. I thought you could deal with the demands of traveling with a child. But if you can't, I'll have to organize something else." The look in her eyes was threatening. As I always did, I backed down. I nodded meekly, put my things down in my room, and then headed back to Aaralyn's suite.

After a night where I had been entertaining Kyle until he finally fell asleep at three a.m., occasionally nodding off myself while he played, while Aaralyn dozed in the comfort of her vast bed, I was up at the crack of dawn. From my window, I could see the Duomo, one of the most famous cathedrals in the world, pigeons flocking outside. But I was more excited about something else: We were walking distance from Via della Spiga and Via Montenapoleone, streets that were filled with the best boutiques in the world.

Aaralyn hadn't told me what she had planned for the day, but I was hoping that I would have at least a little time to wander around on my own. Given everything I had done since leaving Los Angeles, surely that wasn't too much to ask for?

My phone rang at nine.

"Indie, I have a meeting downstairs in an hour. Come and look after Kyle while I get dressed, would you? You can order up some room service when you get here."

I tossed on some clothes and went to Aaralyn's suite, where Kyle was on the floor playing with his Curious George monkey. He smiled at me when I walked in. Aaralyn was already in the shower.

When she emerged, dressed, forty-five minutes later, she looked like the Aaralyn that I had admired. She was in a Dior pantsuit. She had blow-dried her hair straight, and wore nothing but solitaire diamonds in her ears and a simple leather-strap watch.

She looked like she belonged here.

She bent down to kiss Kyle good-bye. But when he realized his mother was going somewhere, he began screeching and clutching at her sleeve.

"It's okay, I'm here," I said, holding him. But he pushed against me and lunged for his mother again.

Aaralyn closed her eyes, a look of dismay on her face.

"Okay, look, just come downstairs with me. As long as he sees me, he's fine. You can sit with us, but just keep him entertained, okay? I don't want any interruptions. It's a very important meeting."

She had made *that* clear yesterday, but I was still excited about being able to go along; at least I'd be seeing *something*, meeting *someone*, instead of being cooped up in an expensive hotel suite with a distressed toddler for company.

We rode the elevator down—given how Aaralyn looked and the way I was now dressed, there could be no confusion about who was who in this relationship—and headed to the lobby lounge. The place smelled of espresso and expensive perfume. The two men that Aaralyn was meeting with showed up soon after we got there. They were both impeccably dressed; slim suits, gorgeous silk ties, thick, masculine watches. Even though I was stuck out in Agoura, I knew that few people in Los Angeles ever dressed like that.

Aaralyn even introduced us, turning on the charm.

"This is my son, Kyle, and my babysitter, Indie," she said. "He had some trouble as I was leaving my room so I thought to bring him along. I hope that's okay. He'll be very quiet."

"Ah, I have two *bambinos* myself," said one of the men, who was introduced to me as Gerardo. "What are we without our children?" he said amiably as Aaralyn nodded in agreement.

Cups of coffee and plates of biscotti were ordered. I was sitting on the farthest end of a long couch, trying to remove myself as much as possible from the proceedings, but unable to avoid completely eavesdropping. Kyle was momentarily content, coloring in his Spider-Man book.

"We have been following your magazine for some time," said Gerardo. "We have been looking to expand our international holdings and this seems like a good match for us. You know, we publish fourteen other lifestyle publications around Europe. In America, we have nothing yet. *Celebrity Style* would be our first."

Aaralyn was smiling. She obviously really wanted to do this. It was probably a dream opportunity for anyone who had founded a magazine from nothing.

"But," said the second man, whose name was Giuseppe. "We have some concerns."

The smile disappeared from Aaralyn's face.

"Our sources in the American media have been telling us that lately, what is happening with *Celebrity Style* is not so good, hmm?" He gestured with his hand, as if trying to drive home his point.

"You have been losing many stories. Is that right? And some advertisers are abandoning you. My colleague Gerardo loves your magazine, the *intelligence* of it. He sees the potential. But I am the money man. I cannot invest in something until I *know* there will be a substantial return. What are you doing to bring your magazine back to its former power?"

This was totally riveting. Kyle was now chewing on a purple crayon and while I made some vague attempt to extract it from his tiny fingers, I was more focused on what was being said at the table. I was actually sitting in on a high-level business dealing. And while I didn't really understand everything that they were saying, I knew enough to know that Aaralyn's future was at stake.

But she had a blank expression on her face. It was a question that she didn't seem to know how to answer.

"I am told," Gerardo continued, "that a popular website in America has been taking all your exclusives. Somehow, they are getting all your information. Maybe we should consider acquiring them?" he asked, raising a neatly groomed eyebrow.

"I assure you, I have that situation under control," Aaralyn said. I knew she was lying. Just last night, it had happened again. Aaralyn was nowhere near to having it under control.

"We will look at the numbers again and make our decision in the next few days," said Giuseppe, rising to indicate that the meeting was over. "We are very grateful that you have taken the time to come and see us, especially with a child," he said, glancing over at Kyle and me. "But this would be an important acquisition for us. We will let you know our decision before you leave."

After they left, Aaralyn remained on the couch, sipping the last of her coffee. She looked worried—more worried than I'd ever seen her. She reached into her bag for her cell phone, maybe wanting to call Juno, before realizing that it would be too late in LA.

She turned to me, her face blank.

"I'm in trouble, Indie," she said.

twenty-four

Her eyes were fixed on mine. Kyle was now scribbling on his Aquadoodle. The place was quiet. It was just Aaralyn Taylor, the woman I had almost worshipped for years, and me. And she was actually talking to me.

"Things are not good," she said. "These problems that you've just heard about—they've been happening for a while. I've tried to keep it under wraps. But I can't. The publishing world is too small. Things get out. But I need this deal to happen."

I knew she was only talking to me because there was nobody else around. It wasn't like she could call Juno or Meghan or anybody else in her office. For the first time since I had met her, Aaralyn Taylor looked completely alone, completely vulnerable.

I didn't know what to say. I thought of telling her how great her magazine was, but that seemed almost silly and of no consequence. She didn't need praise or encouragement from her sixteen-year-old babysitter.

"We've taken some big hits," she continued, almost talking to herself. "Subscriptions are down, advertising has dropped. My cash flow is the worst it's ever been. I shouldn't even be staying at this place, but I thought it would be important to present a good face, to impress these people."

"Yes," I said, nodding sympathetically. "I agree." I paused for a minute. I wanted to say something to her, but I wasn't sure what that should be. Then I decided to just speak from my heart.

"Aaralyn, I know you probably don't really need my opinion. But I just want to tell you that there was a time when *Celebrity Style* was by far the best magazine on the newsstands. Everyone knew it. You've run into some problems lately, but it doesn't mean that you are worth anything less. You are still the best editor out there. I know everything is going to be all right."

"Thanks," said Aaralyn. "You're a very sweet girl."

I felt like I was twelve again.

"Look, it's a gorgeous day and we're in Milan. So why don't we go out and enjoy ourselves?" she said.

Finally.

We were on the Via della Spiga. Kyle was in his stroller, asleep. I was gazing at the Victorian architecture, the stone buildings, the pigeons that flew overhead and landed on the cobbled streets. I was surrounded by Prada and Gucci, Yves Saint Laurent and Dolce & Gabbana, Alexander McQueen and Tod's. The sun was out. People rushed by, smoking cigarettes and chatting on cell phones, a whirl of navy suits and knotted ties and sashaying linens. Tiny cars squeezed into even tinier spaces. My platform shoes clicked against the unevenly paved streets.

I was in heaven.

Aaralyn was window-shopping, talking as she went, telling me about the first time she had come to Milan to see the fashion shows. She was still a student then, but loved fashion as much as she did today. She had taken a cheap flight, stayed in an out of the way hotel, and waited at the entrances to the shows begging for an extra ticket. She wandered through these streets then as she was doing now, gazing through the windows, hoping that one day she would be able to walk in and buy anything she wanted.

"That day finally came," she said, standing in front of the Narciso Rodriguez boutique. Then she turned to look at me. "I don't want those days to end. I *need* this."

I nodded, not knowing what to say.

"Come on, let's go get some lunch," she said.

We went to Bice, which Aaralyn told me was one of her favorite restaurants in Milan and one she always made an effort to stop at when she was here.

"Everybody comes here," she said, mentioning names

to me I had only ever read about: Tom Ford, Donatella Versace, lots of Hollywood stars. "We may as well enjoy the good life while we can," she said, ordering a glass of chianti.

She ordered warm antipasti and breaded veal, some pasta for Kyle, and I went for eggplant and cheese. Her mood seemed a bit improved but I could tell she was still preoccupied. But at least, amid the clatter of the lunchtime crowd, she continued talking to me, telling me about her experiences in Milan and in Paris, about the people she had met. It was almost as if there was a part of her that was almost preparing to say good-bye to this lifestyle. We were bonding! It almost didn't matter how Aaralyn had treated me in the past—because she was treating me as an equal now.

Halfway through lunch, I could tell that Kyle needed a diaper change. I picked him up out of his high chair and took him into the ladies' room. I pulled out the changing table, laid down one of the disposable cloths we always carried around, and placed him gently on it.

Two women were talking behind closed cubicle doors.

"They're offering five million," said one in a strong New York accent. "It's a good chunk of change for a day's work."

"Yeah, but I don't want to jump on that bandwagon. I'm better than that," said an English-accented woman. "Nicole Kidman, Gwyneth Paltrow, Halle Berry—they're all on that endorsement thing. I said I'd never do it. And I never will."

I was trying to concentrate on Kyle, but what was being said behind those closed doors was far more fascinating. Who were these women?

Both doors opened at almost the same time. Behind one was someone I didn't recognize. But behind the other was Chiara Baird, the British actress who was one of Hollywood's "it" girls. Her mother was a famous Sicilian opera singer, her father a noted British playwright. She had burst on to the Hollywood scene just a few months ago, in a lead role in a small independent movie that all the critics had loved. Because of her stunning good looks and acting chops, she was one of the most sought-after young actresses of the moment. But she had managed to stay enigmatic and mysterious, limiting her public engagements, not doing interviews, avoiding those red carpet events. Everyone wanted to dress her, but she liked wearing clothes that she would find in little thrift stores. She was always beautifully put together, but refused to do the designer thing.

They looked at me as they washed their hands, suddenly realizing that maybe they should stop talking. But I needed them to continue. I could sense that there was a story here. I had to think quickly.

"Cute baby," the New York woman said, smiling at me.

"Sorry, no English," I replied, in the heaviest Indian

accent I could muster. I sounded like one of my grandmothers. Then I turned to Kyle, and started speaking Hindi, telling him in my parent's native tongue that "the world was round, the sky was blue, the sun was pretty and so are you." I had no idea what I was saying. All I knew was that I sounded ridiculous. But Chiara and the other woman suddenly looked relaxed. They could continue speaking.

"Luca Berlutti is being called the next Armani," the woman said, now reapplying her lipstick. "He's got a huge amount of backing and doesn't dress just anybody. The fact that he wants you to be his new spokesmodel is major. As your agent, I'm telling you: You've been working in Hollywood less than a year. Five million dollars for a few days' work shooting a campaign? It's unheard of."

"You've just got your eye on your fifteen percent, haven't you?" Chiara said, grinning. "That's okay. You don't have to deny it."

"Chiara, look at what it would mean. They'll fly you to Milan twice a year, put you up at the Four Seasons and wine and dine you endlessly. You will never have to buy another piece of clothing in your life. And, quite frankly, with five million in the bank, you don't have to make another movie for a couple of years."

"But I *like* making movies," she said. "I just don't want to be seen as another commodity. That's all."

"It's Hollywood and it's fashion and you're young and beautiful," said her agent. "Trust me. You're already a commodity. Luca's people want to know by three today. Are we on board?"

Chiara stared at herself in the mirror, smoothing an eyebrow. Even in the harsh bathroom lighting, she was exquisite. I was trying not to stare and realized that with all my wiping and swiping, Kyle's bottom was probably the cleanest it had ever been.

"Okay, Judy, fine. Whatever you say. But if it backfires and I become just another overexposed harlot, it'll be on your head."

As soon as they walked out, I dressed Kyle again, gathered our things, and followed them. Aaralyn, who had moved on to coffee and dessert already, saw them from across the room.

"Look," she said, gesturing in their direction. "That's Chiara Baird." She frowned. "I wonder what she's doing in town."

"Aaralyn," I said, trying to keep my voice down and my palpitations to a minimum. "You're not going to *believe* what I just heard."

As soon as I had told Aaralyn what I had overheard in the bathroom, she had immediately called Meghan. Then Aaralyn got out her phone book and called Luca Berlutti's publicist and Chiara Baird's agent. By the following afternoon, and at least twenty phone calls later, she had the story confirmed: Chiara Baird, hot young Hollywood actress, was going to be the new face of Luca Berlutti, hot young Italian fashion designer. It was a marriage made in heaven.

The morning we were leaving, Giuseppe and Gerardo came back to the hotel for another meeting. They had somber looks on their faces. The news didn't look good.

"Before you say anything, I would like to share something with you," said Aaralyn, once we were ensconced in a corner table. She had a glow in her face. Suddenly she looked youthful and almost carefree. I could almost imagine her as a young fashion journalist, just starting out, relishing every scoop. It was like she was reliving that again.

"On Friday, the latest issue of *Celebrity Style* comes out. On the cover will be a story that even your best journalists here in Italy have been unable to get." Aaralyn told Giuseppe and Gerardo about the Baird-Berlutti alliance.

"We will be breaking the news, a worldwide exclusive," she said proudly.

"But how?" Gerardo asked.

Aaralyn looked at me. Because she had opened up to me so much earlier, I figured that she would have no qualms telling her potential investors that the story had come through me. I straightened my posture, getting ready to finally be noticed by them.

"Oh, let's just say I have my ways," she said, turning away from me.

A cool chill came over me.

"Anyway," she continued. "I can assure you that this scoop will put my magazine back on top. By Friday afternoon, all the entertainment shows will be calling me. Everyone will be talking about *Celebrity Style*.

The two Italians looked at each other. Gerardo reached into his briefcase and pulled out a thick sheaf of papers.

"Well, then," he said, taking a slow sip of his coffee. "Maybe we have a deal."

twenty-five

Given my career-saving coup, I was hoping that Aaralyn would at least upgrade me to first class, that even though she obviously had trouble giving recognition to anyone other than herself, she could at least thank me privately.

But there was no such thing on her part.

Instead, Aaralyn, Kyle, and I sat in near silence in the first-class lounge before our flight. And once we got on board, she went her way, and Kyle and I went ours.

Aldo wasn't at the airport, surprisingly. Instead, there was another driver, Jimmy, who told us that Aldo was sick. He was going to first whisk Aaralyn and Kyle to their home, and then me back to mine. In Aaralyn's bag was a copy of the contract that the Italians had handed her. She was going to show it to her lawyers and send it back. But as she had said to them before leaving, there was no reason the deal wouldn't go through.

I got home exhausted. My mother flung her arms

around me as if I had been missing for six years, and my father's first question was how I had been treated by Aaralyn.

"Fine, Dad," I said. "It was amazing," not pointing out that today was June 15. The day I was once so sure I'd get a phone call from *Celebrity Style*.

After giving me a day to recover, they asked me about my plans for the rest of the summer.

"Mohit's daughters are still keen that you go with them. They're leaving for India in two weeks. We can apply for your visa tomorrow," my father said.

"But Dad," I started to protest.

He didn't want to hear it, holding up his hand to tell me so.

"Indie, need I remind you that you made a promise before you left? You told me that if I let you go to Italy, that you would give up on these crazy ideas and do something more useful with your summer," he said. "Can you imagine how it will look on your application to Harvard, when you mention that you spent two months in India serving the poor and destitute?"

He was right. I *had* promised. And being the good Indian girl I was, a promise had to be kept.

The cover was beautiful. Across the whole front page of *Celebrity Style* was a recent photograph of Chiara Baird, wearing a Luca Berlutti bias-cut chiffon gown. Underneath it was a large white caption: LUCA BERLUTTI'S FIVE MILLION DOLLAR GIRL.

I turned to the inside page, which said FULL STORY. All the details were there, everything I'd overheard in the bathroom in Milan that day, plus background that a staff writer had put together. I narrowed my eyes and peered at the bottom of the page. Sometimes, these stories came with an "Additional reporting by" byline. I thought that perhaps, in some bizarre showing of good grace on her part, Aaralyn might have put my name there. But there was nothing. I tried to tell myself that I had had a wonderful free trip to Milan, as a companion to a woman I had admired from afar for years. I tried to tell myself that it had all been worth it.

But there was a feeling gnawing away inside me that contradicted that. I felt used and disrespected. Honestly, I thought to myself: That's the last time I help out Aaralyn Taylor. Ever.

The "inkys" and I were flying to Calcutta on the afternoon of June 30, the day before the internship job would actually start. I wondered who it was that had landed it, assuming it was probably Brooke. I had been so numb about everything that had happened lately that I didn't even care anymore. It was really over.

Plus, I couldn't think about that now. I had a twenty-two-hour flight in front me, with changes in Tokyo and

Bangkok, with the "inkys" for company. I had to steel myself. I had to pack plenty of reading material. I had to psych myself up to go off and do something that, in my heart of hearts, I just didn't want to do.

As I was drowning in a mountain of clothes, trying to figure out what to take, my mother came in with a cup of freshly brewed chai, a cinnamon stick protruding from the creamy beige liquid.

"Here," she said, handing it over. "Need any help?" she continued, looking over at the mounds of garments on my bed.

"No, Mom, thanks. I just want to make sure I have enough. Two months is a long time."

"Yes, it is, my darling," she said, her head cocked to one side, her eyes wistful. "We shall miss you tremendously."

"Oh, I just remembered something," she said, suddenly straightening up. "I found something while you were gone. I thought this was very interesting." She led me to my computer, sat down at the chair, and logged on to a website.

"What are you doing, Mom?" I asked, astonished, as she typed in the words GossipAddict.com. "Since when are you interested in that kind of thing? How did you even know about it?"

"Oh," she said, turning around to look up at me. "You know, the day after you left for Milan, I was doing Google to find a remedy for my chapped lips. They were very dry. Do you remember?"

I shook my head inattentively.

"But I saw you had just been on some GossipAddict.com site. So even I thought I would see what it was. I found something very interesting on there."

She went to a link on the home page under "Who We Are." She opened it up and showed me a photograph. Two women, who had given themselves the pen names Patsy and Edina. As in *Absolutely Fabulous*. They were sisters who had the much more ordinary real-life names of Emma and Tracy. One was a former television writer, another a beauty editor, but realized their "love for gossip overpowered all else." They were seated at desks in what looked like a busy office, some people milling around behind them. I would never have given it a second thought.

"Look," said my mother, pointing to a shadowy figure in the background.

I gasped.

"Oh my God, Mom," I said. "Do you know what you've found? It all makes sense now."

I pressed PRINT on my computer.

My mother had loaded me down with so much luggage that I looked like a coolie. She figured that just because I was the only one in the family going to India didn't mean that I couldn't carry a colossal amount of gifts for relatives there.

The night before, right after my mother had shown me what she had discovered, I picked up the phone to call Aaralyn. I wanted to tell her that my mother had recognized Aldo in the background of a photograph on the GossipAddict.com site, that my mother remembered him from when he had come to pick me up on the day we had flown to Milan. She had trusted him all this time and he had betrayed her. He had driven her around, listening to all her phone conversations, and fed the information to a competing news source.

But before I dialed her number, I stopped. Why should I bother? She had certainly expressed no gratitude or appreciation so far for anything else I'd done for her in the past. She had met my attempts at goodwill, at showing her my concern, with a stony self-absorption. Maybe I should just let her go down.

If I were anybody else, that's exactly what I would have done.

But I wasn't anybody else. I was just me, Indira Rajiv Konkipuddi, the daughter of a neurosurgeon and a homemaker (and sometime detective). I was a girl who loved fashion and was conflicted about so many things.

I recalled my grandfather telling me once on my last trip to India that one of the core teachings in the Hindu scriptures was of a "sincere desire to be of service to others."

"Do something because it is the right and honorable

thing to do, not for any reward you might receive as a result," he said, stroking my head. "In most instances in your life, you will find that performing acts of kindness and mercy bring their own rewards."

Until today, I had never really understood what he was trying to tell me. But at least now, I knew this: Whatever Aaralyn chose to do with the information was her responsibility. I couldn't control if or how she thanked me. This wasn't about recognition. It was about being a dutiful person. And I, Indira Konkipuddi, was all about duty.

So I called her.

"He's been working for me for two years," she said, once I relayed what my mother had discovered. "I can't believe it."

She paused. "Well, thanks for letting me know." And she hung up.

"You have everything *beta?*" my father asked. I checked my tote to make sure all my water purification tablets and Power Bars were in there. Eight weeks with the "inkys" were going to be hard enough without having to endure Delhi-belly.

Kim had come over to see me off, and she and I stood on the pavement outside my house, saying good-bye. She had also come to tell me that she and Brett had broken up. She didn't seem too distraught over it, though.

"I guess the fantasy Brett was better than the real Brett," she said, laughing. "I've downloaded a new ring tone, by the way."

As my father loaded the last of my luggage into his car, a BMW pulled up.

To my astonishment, out stepped Aaralyn. She reached into the backseat and pulled out Kyle. He lunged for me when he saw me.

"Dindy," he squealed. *"Dindy!"* Aaralyn was holding him, but he was looking straight at me.

"Indie, I've been trying to reach you," she said, walking up the driveway. "I'm glad I caught you."

"Oh, sorry, Aaralyn. I've just been so busy preparing for this trip to India that I haven't checked my voice mail since yesterday, and before that . . ."

My father interjected.

"You must be Miss Taylor. It is a pleasure to meet you at last," he said, extending his hand to her. "But I'm afraid your timing is somewhat faulty. Indie here will miss her flight. Departure is on schedule."

I could tell by the way he spoke that he was nervous and that made me feel suddenly sympathetic and strangely loyal. For all his medical degrees and professional success, my father was an unassuming man, and I could see that Aaralyn unnerved him.

"How did you even know I was leaving today?" I asked.

"You told me in Milan that you had promised your

dad you would spend the summer in India if he let you accompany me. Don't you remember? You said you would have exactly two weeks back before having to fly off again. I didn't get to where I am by easily forgetting things. I called last night on your home number. Your father told me you were flying out today. Didn't he give you the message?"

I spun my head around to look at my father, who had a rather sheepish expression on his face.

"Sorry, Indie," he said. "I knew you were busy preparing for your trip and didn't want to distract you."

I knew my father was lying. He had been so thrilled when I had agreed to go away to India for the summer, that he must have been terrified that a single phone call from Aaralyn was going to demolish all that. He figured that all she would have to do was beckon me and I would go running to her. A few weeks ago, he might have been right. But I didn't want to be Aaralyn's puppet anymore.

I think the look in my eyes told her as much. We all stood there awkwardly, wondering what Aaralyn was going to say next. I still had no idea why she was here. But I wasn't about to ask her. I had made enough overtures to her in the past. Now, it was her turn.

I set my bag down. I cast a thoughtful look her way, just the faintest glimmer of a smile on my face, wanting to dilute any tension. A small part of me wanted to say something to her—to remind her of all I had done for her and the fact that I had never really been thanked for it. Not even once. I wanted to tell her how upset I had been, how my self-confidence had been shattered. I wanted to share with her that she had been my idol for years, that I aspired to be like her when I grew up, but I saw now that she wasn't the woman I had created in the fantasy fashion land that had occupied my head.

But of course I knew I wouldn't say any of this. Not only was confrontation of any sort just not my thing, but my parents were standing by, monitoring every word, every inflection. I just didn't want to embarrass myself in their eyes.

"Indie," Aaralyn said finally, taking a step toward me. "I know when we first met, the day you ran after my limo, you wanted that internship at my magazine," she said.

I felt my stomach lurching, as if I were being flung forward in a fast car. My heart was pounding. This was the first time she had ever even brought up the subject of the internship. My immediate thought was that she had realized the error of her ways, that she had dismissed me too early. The deadline had passed, but maybe she was going to give it to me, anyway—in person.

"I said then I couldn't give it to you," Aaralyn continued, biting her bottom lip, something that made her look suddenly fragile and vulnerable. "And I'm sorry, Indie, but I'm saying the same thing today. It's gone to Brooke."

Everything around me suddenly came screeching to

a halt. The blood rose to my cheeks. How stupid I continued to be! When would I ever learn?

"That's okay, Aaralyn," I said. "It was something I really, really wanted, but I think I knew a long time ago that you would never give it to me. I mean, I'm not really the kind of person who could ever get a job at your magazine, am I?"

We were standing next to a busy bougainvillea plant, its bright fuchsia blooms contrasting with Aaralyn's dove-gray dress. That was the only thing I could focus on, the only stopping me from crying in front of her.

My parents both looked uncomfortable. I knew my mother was tempted to break the tension with an offer of freshly baked walnut muffins and coffee. But she didn't offer food.

"Miss Taylor. May I say something?" my mother asked. She came to my side and put her arm across my shoulders.

"Our Indie, she has done so much for you," my mother said quietly. "And she has asked for nothing in return. We have never quite understood her fascination with this fashion thing, but we have always respected her and chosen to support her. But I must say, Miss Taylor, your mistreatment of our daughter has saddened me enormously. We are both mothers after all. Our children are everything. We would die to protect them from hurt. Surely you agree?"

Aaralyn flinched. She looked over at Kyle, who was

sitting on our grassy front lawn and was quite content pulling petals of daisies and laying them on the top of his head.

Then Aaralyn shut her eyes for a second. Her eyelids were dusted with beige shimmer powder. Even in the bright morning sun, her skin was flawless. But beneath the perfect veneer, she looked troubled.

"Mrs. Konkipuddi, Indie, that's one of the reasons I am here today," she said. Her voice was almost whisper-quiet, and completely lacking in the harsh undertone she had almost always spoken to me in.

"Apart from telling you about Brooke, there's something more important. After I fired Aldo yesterday, I lay in bed all night and realized, with momentous regret, that I have never thanked you. Not for anything. Not for the sensational job you have been doing with Kyle and for all the immeasurable things you did for me and my magazine. That Trixie Van Alden story. Then Luca Berlutti, which was the scoop that got my magazine sold and set me up for life. And, of course, finding out about Aldo."

"That bit was my mother," I said, smiling more fully now.

"You have to understand something about me, Indie. I have always fought to be in control. I have always wanted to be at the top of my game. I have never wanted to admit that I needed help from anyone. And then you come along, a teenage babysitter with no work experience, and you help me in ways I could never have imagined. It was all a bit too much for me to comprehend. I just didn't want to admit that I had failed in so many ways. It left me feeling so inadequate."

My heart swelled at hearing something from Aaralyn that sounded so poignantly truthful.

"And Indie, before I go, there's just one other thing," she said.

"When I came to your school, you were the first one to stand up and ask me a question. You remember that, don't you?"

"Yes, of course, Aaralyn. How could I forget?"

"Your question was about what a person needed to get into this business. I told you the only truth I know: that it takes connections and contacts. I stand by that.

"But," she continued, now putting her hand on my arm, "if there's anybody who can make it without those connections, Indie, it's you. You live for fashion and those are the people who always make it in this business, connections or not. You are passionate about it and, more than that, you're smart about it. Do you know how rare that it is? And, beyond all that, you have a grace and courtesy beyond your years, an utter lack of guile. I do hope you'll go where your dreams take you, Indie."

My father had heard every word and nodded.

"We'll see," I said, my voice steady and resolute. "But

right now I have a plane to catch."

"Well, I'd better get back to the office," Aaralyn replied brusquely. "Brooke is out lunching at The Ivy and wants to spend the afternoon following Paris Hilton around Kitson." At that, she rolled her eyes.

"Oh, and by the way," she said. "Cayman called from camp this morning. He says to say hi. He's going to e-mail you in India."

I smiled. It was going to be a fun summer after all.

Aaralyn extended her hand toward me, reconsidered for a second, and then leaned in to hug me.

"Next summer, maybe?" she asked.

"Next summer," I replied.

She put Kyle in his car seat, got into her car, and drove off.

And this time, I knew I didn't have to run after it.

Kavita Daswani has been a fashion correspondent for CNN International and CNBC Asia, and has written for the *Los Angeles Times*, among many other publications. Her first adult novel, *For Matrimonial Purposes*, was hailed as a "cross-cultural confection" by *People* magazine, as "delightful" by *USA Today*, and as "Bridget Jones with a distinct Indian flavor" by *School Library Journal*. *Booklist* called her novel *The Village Bride of Beverly Hills* "a thoughtful romantic comedy." And Jennifer Weiner raved that *Salaam, Paris*, Kavita's third adult novel, is "the perfect blend of real-life drama and fairy-tale whimsy."

Kavita lives with her husband and two sons in Los Angeles, where she writes for *Women's Wear Daily* and *Vogue India*. She makes her YA debut with *Indie Girl*.

PULSE it

ook?

e?

Log on to
www.SimonSaysTEEN.com
to find out how you can get
free books from **Simon Pulse**
and become part of our **IT Board**,
where you can tell **US**, what **you** think!

SIMON
PULSE